Sins of the Fathers

by

Catherine Sue Morgan

This is a work of fiction. Names, characters, places, and incidents are either the product of the author's imagination or are used fictitiously, and any resemblance to actual persons living or dead, business establishments, events, or locales, is entirely coincidental.

Sins of the Fathers

Cover Art by *RJ Morris*

The Wild Rose Press, Inc.
PO Box 708
Adams Basin, NY 14410-0708
Visit us at www.thewildrosepress.com

Publishing History
First Crimson Rose Edition, 2015
Print ISBN 978-1-5092-0220-1
Digital ISBN 978-1-5092-0221-8

Published in the United States of America

Thanks to years of morbid curiosity, of observing from a distance and following his career with a gruesome fascination, Becca recognized Jack Conroy instantly.

Caught, she thought, and her breath jammed up in her throat until she was so lightheaded she had to grab the doorframe to keep her balance.

"This gentleman is here to see you. Becca," Denise announced. "I was just about to buzz."

Breathe, she told herself.

He turned and took a step in her direction, slowed, and then took another step. His wide shoulders seemed to take up the whole waiting room, and the last brilliant rays of the sun streaming through the window glinted gold in his hair as he strode toward her, an avenging angel, come to mete out justice. His face was all rough planes and sharp angles, with high cheekbones, thin lips, and a square jaw that might have been chiseled out of stone. She fought the urge to flee, and then it was too late.

Dedications

Dedicated to my mother,
Lorna Jones Morgan,
who believed in me to her last breath.
And to my critique partners,
including my sister, Mary Jane Morgan,
Karen Crane, Loulou Harrington, Emrys Moreau,
Catie McGoldrick (miss you, Catie),
Margaret Daley, and Laura Marie Altom.

Prologue

He stood in the shadows, watching and waiting.

The snow was coming down hard and fast, coating the frozen ground, outlining the bare trees, accumulating on parked cars. It covered his jacket and drifted against his boots.

A lesser man might be shivering, but he'd learned early in life to control the flesh, to rise above pain and discomfort. He'd had a powerful teacher.

He tensed in anticipation at the sound of an approaching car. It passed slowly, an elderly man at the wheel, and he relaxed again, hoped the old guy made it safely to his destination. Somewhere nearby a fire burned in a fireplace; he could smell the smoke in the clean, cold air.

He took what fate delivered to him. He'd never have chosen this one. She looked barely out of childhood and innocent. But appearances could be deceiving, as he well knew, and he couldn't have received a clearer sign. It had been a trinity of fives.

Another car and this one slowed, pulled into the driveway. She made no move to get out. He reined in a jolt of impatience. He'd waited over an hour. He could be patient another few minutes.

Finally she climbed out of the car and circled to the

back, opened the trunk, and leaned in. Time to make his move.

He slipped out of his hiding place and crept up behind her, moving quickly and soundlessly. He had a gloved hand over her mouth and his knife at her throat before she knew anything was amiss.

She struggled in his arms, but she was no match for his superior strength. He closed the trunk lid with an elbow, kicked the packages she'd dropped underneath the car and out of sight. She weighed hardly anything, and he easily dragged her to the darkest side of the house.

He eased the pressure of his hand on her mouth, felt her take in a deep breath. The bitch! He slammed her face into the brick siding before she could scream. She groaned and fell to her knees.

He forced her onto her back, onto the snow covered ground, and straddled her. In the moonlight reflected off the snow, he could see that her eyes were swelling shut. Her nose hung crookedly on her face. Her skin was a mottled reddish purple. *Now* the ugly inside her was showing. He smiled in satisfaction.

"Don't," she whispered. "Please don't."

He pressed the tip of the knife to her mouth in warning. That shut her up. Fascinated, he watched the blood well up on her lip. He nicked her again and observed the blood bubble from that cut. She whimpered. Furious, he backhanded her.

"You know you want it." He slashed and ripped at her clothes, stripped them aside. With one hand he unsnapped his jeans, fumbled with the zipper.

"No," she mumbled, shaking her head. "No."

He squeezed her throat until she quieted and went

limp. He dragged the knife down and then across her left breast. The sight of the bloody cross made him harder, drove him higher. Now he was going to teach the whore a lesson.

Chapter One

Thursday, February 2nd

Kevin had disappeared again. Becca pictured him huddled under a bridge somewhere. Digging through trash bins. Scavenging cigarette butts from gutters. Alone and frightened and at the mercy of the voices.

There were weeks, even months, she didn't think about the early years at all. During those times she'd always been Rebecca Bennett, well loved daughter of Marie and Charles Bennett, a safe and secure little girl who'd grown into a competent and confident woman.

But when Kevin took off, it was right there, just below the surface, all the time, as close as the network of veins beneath her skin. And then a client would say or do some little something and without warning a vein would burst, spilling a memory into her conscious mind. The sharp crack of shattering glass. Big hands, curled tight and swinging hard. The twin scents of sweat and rage, blood and terror. Kevin's screams. Mama's face. Her own whimpers. The tingling sensations in her arms and legs as the paralyzing drug of fear pumped through her, freezing her in place.

Becca jerked her attention back to the pale young woman trembling in the chair across from her, thin arms wrapped tightly around her own torso as if she might shake apart at any minute. The man who'd beaten and raped her was short and thick, dark. Kevin was short, only a few inches taller than her own five-three, with eyes and hair as dark as hers. But Kevin was thin, painfully so. Almost gaunt. Still, to his victim, wouldn't an assailant seem bigger than he actually was?

"Breathe," Becca said, speaking as much to herself as to Lauren. The ugly images faded as she slowly drew in a lungful of air, held it, exhaled, repeated the sequence twice more. Calm again, she eased the ghost of Millard Harrison to the distant past. And the terrified little Becky Harrison with him. For the rest of the therapy hour, she was once again twenty-eight-year-old Rebecca Ann Bennett, licensed clinical social worker, helping victims of violence put their lives back together.

The second Lauren left, Becca started packing up her briefcase. A few minutes later, her receptionist appeared in the doorway.

"Want to go with me to the Caravan? I saw a gorgeous guy there last week. I think he's my soul mate." Denise McAfee fluttered her fingers over her heart and grinned. "Maybe he has a friend. Or have you found someone new to cuddle up with on these cold winter nights?"

Becca rolled her eyes and ignored Denise's none-too-subtle hint that she should be replacing Stan Marshall in her life. Farthest thing from her mind, but she didn't want to talk about what *was* on her mind. Not to Denise, not to anyone.

"Starting tonight, I'm filling in for Eileen as the rape-victim support group leader, remember?"

"Oh, right. Well, I'm off." Denise jangled her car keys. "Wish me luck."

Forty-two and twice divorced, Denise was on a mission to find a man. Hence the bleached blonde hair and the form fitting jeans, the clingy V-neck sweater that showed a little cleavage. Becca worried that Denise's hunt for a man was going to get her in over her head again one of these days, but she'd long ago given up trying to save Denise from herself.

As driven as Denise was to find a man, Becca was even more desperate to find her brother and save *him* from himself. Save her brother, thereby saving her mother and her niece and maybe even herself. She opened her middle desk drawer, grabbed a granola bar, and dropped it into her purse.

Abruptly she stood and shrugged into her coat. She had an hour before group started. She had time to check out the soup kitchen on Denver. Who knew, maybe she'd find Kevin there tonight and end this nightmare.

As she pulled on her gloves, a sliver of guilt worked its way through her. A blanket of snow and ice covered the city of Tulsa. Temperatures, especially at night, were lethal. The shelters had run out of room and were turning people away. Her brother was out there somewhere, while she was warm and dry.

He'd been gone for over a month. She'd spent the last thirty-two days looking for him: driving the deserted streets late at night; stopping by the Salvation Army shelter early, on her way to work; checking at the Day Center for the Homeless on her lunch hour. All day Saturday she crisscrossed downtown, scanning the faces turned raptly to the sidewalk preachers, peered down alleys, and canvassed the familiar haunts of the homeless. On Friday evening she volunteered at the soup kitchen, and Sunday afternoon she volunteered at the Day Center.

She touched base with her buddy Larry Driscoll at the Salvation Army shelter early in the morning, hoping that Kevin had come in from the cold the night before and might still be there. She called David Anderson at the Day Center every day after work to see if Kevin had come in during the afternoon. She checked with Joe Bonner at the soup kitchen every evening on whether Kevin had come through the line for dinner. Several times Joe had called her to tell her that Kevin was there, but by the time Becca had gotten downtown he'd always been gone. He'd been in the Day Center multiple times, but always during times when she was seeing clients. As far as she knew, he had yet to seek refuge overnight at the Salvation Army shelter.

Stifling a yawn, she stepped out into the damp, frigid air and locked the office door behind her. Carefully, she navigated down the slick steps and across the parking lot to her Honda Civic. She tossed the briefcase into the trunk and climbed inside. Time to resume her search. Kevin had once been her protector, and now she was his.

She knew what was in his head, what he'd witnessed day in and day out for ten years, the final horror before Charles Bennett had given them new lives. If all that got mixed up with the voices, what would he do?

That was the question that kept her up nights. What would he do?

She had to find him.

****

Jack Conroy turned into the parking lot outside Fitness for Life and scanned the near-empty area for

Mike Sullivan's black Ford Taurus. By habit they worked out together three nights a week. Sully wasn't here yet. Jack pulled into an empty space close to the front door of the health club.

A thirty-something blonde, accompanied by a preteen girl who looked just like her, emerged from the building. The woman cast a worried glance at the sky and leaned down to pull her daughter's scarf closer around her neck. When they drew even with him she slowed and stared, then hurried past him, keys in one hand, a firm grip on her daughter with the other.

The girl tossed a wary glance at him over her shoulder as she scurried behind her mother to the car. *Good girl*. If Megan had been more cautious, she might have lived past her eighth year. A picture of Megan the last time he'd seen her, before Millard Harrison had happened on her, came unbidden into his mind. Rage spiked through him, a hot, fast charge of it. He clamped it down.

Suddenly he needed to feel the burn in his muscles as he lifted the weights. He needed to push his body to its limits, clear his mind of everything but the next breath, sweat out the anger that had been building in him all day. Sully would show up or he wouldn't.

Jack turned his truck off, hunched his shoulders against the cold and stepped outside. Snow and ice crunched under his boots as he crossed the pavement.

The lunatic they were hunting had raped another woman last night. Used his knife on this one. *Really* used it, way beyond the mark on her left breast with which he'd branded all his victims. He'd damn near killed her.

A victim a week for five weeks, each more

brutalized than the last. He *would* kill the next one; Jack knew it in his gut. He and Sully had put in hours and hours of leg work, and they were no closer to catching him than they'd been a month ago, when the son of a bitch had first started out.

Over the last five weeks, they had talked to every known sack of shit pervert in the city of Tulsa. They'd started with those who used knives in their attacks and expanded the focus to include those who used weapons of any kind. Then they'd included the ones who'd been especially violent, with or without weapons. After that they'd enlarged the search to include every man who'd been arrested and/or charged and/or been found guilty of rape, attempted rape, or sexual assault. So far, they hadn't waded through the peepers or the flashers.

They'd interviewed, followed up and checked out alibis, and come up empty handed. They'd done door-to-doors and talked to every neighbor of every victim, talked to family members and friends, chased after every lead, and still they had nothing.

His gut told him that this unsub had been flying low, under the radar screen, for years, perfecting his skills. Although Nancy Rojas had been his first known victim, the attack on her had been well planned and executed. This wasn't an opportunistic rapist. He selected his victims ahead of time. He probably already had another woman in his sights. Jack fisted his hands in frustration.

Now Juliet Crouch, a nineteen-year-old sophomore at the University of Tulsa, lay in a coma at St. Theresa Hospital. Her brain was still swelling, a result of multiple blows to the head. Dozens of knife wounds scarred her body, her nose lay off-center in her face, split open like a baked potato. She had three broken ribs, a mangled left hand, and a punctured right lung. Her family had gathered together in the waiting room outside the ICU, keeping vigil. The silent plea in her parents' eyes that he find the man who'd hurt their daughter and bring him to justice was burning a hole in him.

Twelve years on the force, the last nine in sex crimes/homicide, and sometimes they still got tangled up in his mind with the monster who had raped and killed his sister. At least that son of a bitch was dead. This one was very much alive. Whoever he was, wherever he was, Jack vowed to himself that he'd find him.

****

Becca straightened the folding legs of the long table and locked them in place. She took one end of the table and Georgie Burcham, grandmother of five, crisis line volunteer, co-facilitator of the group and rape survivor, took the other end. Together they flipped the table upright and then wrestled it away from the wall and back into the middle of the room.

"Whew. Furniture moving wears a body out." Georgie swiped a Lucille Ball-red curl off her forehead. "Gimme one last cup of that coffee before you clean the pot, will you, hon?"

Becca poured two cups, dumped the grounds, and rinsed out the carafe before settling into an orange plastic chair.

"How many more babies you think Eileen is going to pop out?" Becca asked. She and Georgie had done the group together two and a half years ago when Eileen had had her first.

"I dunno. My advice is, have a houseful. They grow up awfully fast."

Becca thought with longing of a houseful of children, then shoved the thought away. "So, how do you think it went?"

"Really well. That's the first time Katy has said more than two words. I think the talking did her good. Liked what you said to her."

At fifteen, Katy was the youngest member of the group. She'd sneaked out late at night to go to a party and downed a couple of vodkas to fit in, with disastrous results.

"It was my own fault," she'd insisted after telling her story. "I was drunk."

"Getting drunk is not a rape-able offense," Becca had answered.

"Noticed the new girl, Shannon, was listening pretty close," Georgie added. Becca had noticed, too.

"The young ones need their own group," Georgie said.

"We've been talking about it in board meetings, hiring a part time person to work strictly with teenagers. Maybe do some education on rape in the schools." Becca took a sip of coffee, grimaced, and set the foam cup aside. "This stuff could strip varnish. The problem, of course, is money."

"Come on, time to go home. You look whupped." Georgie rose to her feet and tugged Becca up. "We'll walk out together, be on the safe side."

Becca locked the door behind them. They walked down the long narrow hall, past the public restroom and the dimly lit snack room with its vending machines, up the short flight of stairs to the basement entrance, and emerged into the parking lot, empty but for their two cars.

She climbed into her Civic, locked the doors, and started the engine. Georgie beeped her horn and waved as she turned out onto Columbia Avenue and up to Twenty-First Street. Becca followed her. She should be looking for Kevin, but she was just so tired.

Anger welled up in her. What the hell did he think he was doing, anyway? Disappearing the day before his birthday and making his family worry themselves sick over him? Their mother had lost almost ten pounds in the weeks he'd been gone. His daughter was crying herself to sleep every night, asking when her daddy was coming home. Could he not even think about his daughter? Would he come home on Saturday to wish Cara a happy birthday? Probably not.

Mentally ill people could be so damned selfish.

Screw it. She jerked the steering wheel right instead of left. Tomorrow she'd start in again, but tonight she was going home and getting some sleep.

****

The voices drifted to him out of the night. *Do it. Do it.*

He ran down the alley, weaving and ducking, trying to lose them. His coat, insulated with newspaper, crackled and swished as he moved. When he came to the Dumpster, he lifted the lid and scrambled over the side. He wedged himself into the corner and pulled his knees up to his chin to make himself a smaller receiver. He had hoped the metal container would interfere with the transmission, but no. He clamped his hands over his ears and hummed loudly, but he could still hear them. *Do it. Do it.*

He banged his head against the side, one, two, three, four, five, rapidly, then paused and listened. Blessed silence. He scooted to the middle of the container and scrunched lower in the refuse, piled the · smelly trash on top of him. It would help keep out the cold.

He avoided people whenever he could because he knew they could hear his thoughts. His case manager had insisted not, but why else did everyone stare at him and then edge away?

Cara would be sleeping soundly by now, curled on her side, her rosy lips slightly parted, her chubby little-girl fingers tangled in Hooligan's fur, the collie's back curved against Cara's stomach. He missed Cara. He missed her bad, but he had to stay away to keep her safe. He would not let the evil touch his daughter.

****

Friday, February 3rd

"I was walking the baby. He was colicky. I heard scratching noises in the kitchen. I didn't even go look. I just thought we had mice. I was going to tell Wayne about it when he got home." Beth Ann Waverly sat, rigid as wrought iron, on the chair facing Becca as she told her story. Her eyes glazed over, and she swayed slightly as she traveled back in time.

"I never saw him. He grabbed me from behind and shoved me, face down, onto the sofa." Her unfocused gaze drifted down and to the left. The muscles in her shoulders and arms tensed and trembled as if against a terrible weight.

"The whole time I was thinking 'Don't smother the baby.' " The fingers on her right hand tapped the arm of the chair in time with her words.

"Don't smother the baby," Beth Ann whispered. Tap, tap, tap, tap. Her eyes drifted closed. "Don't smother the baby." More tapping.

"Are you aware of your fingers?" Becca asked.

"He kept telling me to be quiet. 'Be quiet and do what I say,' " she intoned. Her voiced had deepened, her vowels were rounder and softer, so that "I" became "Ah." "I didn't make a sound. I didn't want to wake my daughter up. I didn't want him to know I had a little girl in the house." Silent tears rolled down her face.

"You protected your children," Becca said. "Your little girl didn't wake up, and your baby wasn't harmed."

Beth Ann's fingers fluttered furiously.

"What are your fingers doing?"

"One, two, three, four," Beth Ann said as she tapped.

"What are your fingers counting?"

"Stitches!" Beth Ann exclaimed. Her eyes popped open. "I told the police he had moles on his left thumb, but they were stitches. Four stitches."

"He sounded southern?" Becca asked.

"Yes." Beth Ann's eyes widened. "Not Texas, that's where I'm from. More like Mississippi or Alabama or Georgia."

"Who's your detective?"

"Jack Conroy. Know him?"

Did she know him? Sure, they were related by blood, in a manner of speaking. Becca nearly lost a nervous giggle but grabbed hold of it before it escaped.

"Not personally, but I've heard of him. He's good," she reassured Beth Ann. "Thorough and persistent. Probably has the highest clear record in the department.

I think you need to tell him about the stitches and the accent."

She hoped and prayed that she never met Jack Conroy face to face. One of her worst fears was that he'd take one look at her and see the eight-year-old she'd been when tragedy had struck his family. She knew the fear was irrational. None of them had ever had their faces in the newspaper or on TV; just her dad. At least, she didn't think so. She'd have to ask her mother.

****

"Thanks, Mrs. Waverly. If you remember anything else, be sure to call me." Jack dropped the receiver in its cradle and stood.

"Gotcha," he muttered under his breath, the thrum of the hunt humming along his nerve endings.

In the door-to-door, he'd interviewed Beth Ann's next door neighbor. Gladys Frankel had offered him chocolate chip cookies still warm from the oven, showed off her brand new carpet, and chattered on about the nice young man from Mobile who, poor thing, had cut his hand while putting that carpet down.

Mrs. Frankel had had the carpet laid the day before Beth Ann Waverly's rape. Jack grabbed his keys, signed out, and headed for his car. He'd pay a visit to Miller Carpet and Tile, the store from which Gladys had purchased her plush white carpet, and find out who that nice young man from Alabama was, and where he'd been Tuesday night.

****

Becca stuffed a half-dozen provider recredentialing applications into her briefcase and stacked an armload of client files on the corner of her desk. She was behind on progress notes, backlogged on treatment plans, and bumping up against the deadlines on renewing her preferred provider status with several major health insurance companies. She was going to have to find the time to get caught up this weekend. If she didn't get those recredentialing applications in the mail soon, she wouldn't have to worry about the rest. That had to be top priority.

But not this evening. Friday was her night to volunteer at the soup kitchen. She smothered the hope that Kevin would come through the line tonight and returned her attention to the mountain of work she had to get done this weekend.

Maybe tomorrow afternoon. No, that was Cara's birthday party. Eight years old. An involuntary shiver rippled across her skin. She'd been eight when... She shook her head. No, she wasn't going to think about that now.

Tomorrow night was the baby shower for Eileen, and she still didn't have a baby gift. Mentally she added a trip to the mall on Saturday morning to her weekend must-do list. Sunday, then. Sunday, no matter what, she'd fill out those recredentialing applications.

Except when was she going to look for Kevin? Her anger of the night before had vanished and been replaced by worry. What was he doing? Was he safe? Was everyone else?

She stifled a yawn. She wished she could sleep all weekend, but obviously she couldn't. She was going to have to figure out a way to get caught up on her work *and* continue her search for Kevin.

Oh, well. She'd sleep after she found her brother.

****

"You have the right to remain silent. Anything you say can and will be used against you in a court of law…"

Alvin Wright was already crying like a baby, big fat tears rolling down his pink cheeks, and Jack hadn't even finished reading him his rights. Jack figured he'd have a signed confession from Beth Ann Waverly's rapist inside an hour.

Maybe not, and no big deal either way. He was sure Wright's prints and the ones in Beth Ann's house would be a match and that the semen recovered in the rape exam would match his DNA. Even without the four stitches in his thumb and the accent, it was a slam dunk.

All in all, a good day's work.

One more piece of shit off the streets. Thanks, in large part, to Rebecca Bennett. He'd never met the woman, but she worked wonders with rape victims. She was probably one of those round, grandmotherly types, who soothed the survivors with cookies and hugs. But several of her clients had retrieved detailed memories that had helped Jack nail their assailants.

God bless the grannies of the world.

****

Buoyed by the sight of Alvin Wright wearing orange and huddling in the corner of a city cell, Jack had driven straight to St. Theresa Hospital.

"Five minutes," the diminutive blonde physician said sternly.

Jack nodded and followed Dr. Markowitz into the Intensive Care Unit, past the nurses' station and into the first room, where a multitude of machines whirred and hissed and clicked. A tangle of clear tubing snaked to the broken body in the hospital bed. One lock of red hair on the pillow provided the only color in the white, sterile room.

"This is Jack Conroy from the Tulsa Police Department, and he has a few questions for you if you still feel up to it," Dr. Markowitz said in a smooth, soft voice.

Juliet Crouch blinked, and Jack stepped forward, into her line of vision. Pale blue eyes, visible through a two-inch gap in the gauze bandages that covered her face and head, fixed on him.

"What can you tell me about the person who did this to you?" Jack asked.

"Man," she rasped. "Black."

"A black male?"

"Clothes."

"The man was wearing black clothes?" Jack clarified.

Juliet nodded and turned her head away from him.

He asked about height, weight, race, identifying marks, unusual speech patterns or accents, and Juliet's response to each question was a weak "Don't know" or a hopeless shrug.

"He had a knife." Jack stated the obvious. "Any other weapons?"

"Just a knife," she whispered. Her shallow breathing, already rapid, accelerated. She gasped for air, and the muscles in her arms and legs twitched as if she were trying to flee. A monitor beeped shrilly.

"Out," Dr. Markowitz barked at Jack. "Now."

Jack moved aside, out of the path of a nurse entering the room at a run, and quietly stepped into the hallway. He turned right instead of left to avoid passing the waiting room in which the Crouch family had taken up a fearful residence.

"Damn," he muttered under his breath as he started down the stairs. He'd learned no more from Juliet Crouch than he had from Nancy Rojas, Andrea Marple, or Ann Wilson, the three other women he believed to be victims of the same rapist, who'd definitely been escalating. Although Juliet Crouch had dozens of knife wounds, Ann Wilson eight, and Rojas and Marple only one, all four of them had deep cuts on their left breasts that resembled the letter "t," or a lopsided "x."

He'd talk to Rojas, Marple, and Wilson again, he decided. What did he have to lose? And he'd see if Sully would repeat the door-to-doors in the three neighborhoods. They had to get a bead on this guy, before he got to another woman.

Unless he deviated from his pattern, he'd strike again in another five days. The urgency Jack had been feeling for the last month intensified. Time was running out.

Because the next woman was going to die.

He flashed back to his recent conversation with Beth Ann Waverly, confident and determined as she provided the information that had led him to Alvin Wright, and kicked himself for not having thought of it earlier.

He glanced at his watch. Not quite four o'clock. He headed to the information desk where he borrowed a telephone directory and looked up the address.

Next stop: Rebecca Bennett.

Chapter Two

Friday, February 3rd

Thanks to years of morbid curiosity, of observing from a distance and following his career with a gruesome fascination, Becca recognized Jack Conroy instantly.

Caught, she thought, and her breath jammed up in her throat until she was so lightheaded she had to grab the doorframe to keep her balance.

"This gentleman is here to see you, Becca," Denise announced. "I was just about to buzz."

Breathe, she told herself.

He turned and took a step in her direction, slowed, and then took another step. His wide shoulders seemed to take up the whole waiting room, and the last brilliant rays of the sun streaming through the window glinted gold in his hair as he strode toward her, an avenging angel, come to mete out justice. His face was all rough planes and sharp angles, with high cheekbones, thin lips, and a square jaw that might have been chiseled out of stone. She fought the urge to flee, and then it was too late.

"Jack Conroy, Tulsa Police Department, Sex Crimes/Homicide Division."

His deep voice rolled right through her. She almost said, "I know, for the last nine years, ever since you made detective," but stopped herself in the nick of time. He closed the distance between them and her professional demeanor kicked in as she automatically shook the hand he extended.

"Rebecca Bennett. How may I help you?"

The texture of his rough palm and calloused fingers simultaneously triggered old fears and a startling, unwanted frisson of awareness.

"May we talk privately?" He tilted his head toward Denise, who watched and listened with open interest. He'd yet to let go of her hand.

"Certainly." She pivoted, effectively freeing herself from his grasp, and led the way down the short hall to her private office. Though he moved as quietly as a big cat, she could feel his presence behind her. Surreptitiously, she rubbed her still tingling palm over the ribbed corduroy of her black slacks to douse the sensation and then balled her hand into a loose fist.

She left the office door open and seated herself in the chair nearest to it. He claimed the matching chair directly across from her.

"First, I want to tell you that we arrested Mrs. Waverly's rapist this afternoon."

"Oh, I'm so glad for Beth Ann," Becca said.

"Might not have happened if you hadn't helped her remember the stitches and the southern accent. I appreciate your telling her to call me with that information."

"You're welcome." That's what had prompted this visit? Why hadn't he just called, if he wanted to thank her? Which he never had before, and Beth Ann wasn't the first client she'd sent back to him with additional details. But he gave no indication that he knew who she was, and he hadn't mentioned Kevin, so she relaxed fractionally.

"As you probably know, we have a serial rapist operating in town right now. I'm hoping you can help me apprehend him."

Panic flared anew within her, making her pulse race and her hands tremble. Did he suspect Kevin? If her brother had committed these horrible crimes—and please, please, don't let it be so—she wanted him caught and stopped as much as Jack Conroy did. The difference was that she'd want him to receive the psychiatric care he so desperately needed instead of being dumped into the general prison population where he'd be tortured by the other inmates as well as the voices. She imagined that Jack Conroy would think Kevin was getting off easy with only torture and mutilation.

"Help how?" she asked carefully.

"I just came from the hospital room of the young woman I believe is the suspect's most recent victim. He really did a job on her. She's lucky to be alive. Unfortunately, either she can't remember, or she's too frightened to be able to provide us with any useful information." He leaned forward in his chair, and his gaze intensified. Determination and frustration radiated off him in thick waves. "Will you go to the hospital and talk with her? You seem to have a way of helping survivors remember details."

Becca's mind raced. She drew in another calming breath. Would she help a rape victim? Any time, any place. And what could it hurt if she were to develop a strictly professional relationship with Jack Conroy? If the rapist he was after turned out to be her brother, she'd be in a better position to advocate treatment for him.

"Have you discussed this with her?"

"Not yet. I wanted to find out first if you ever made, ah, house calls, and if you'd do it."

"I'll be glad to go to the hospital, if she wants to see me. It has to be her choice. Choice and control are vital for a person who's had trauma."

"I'll go ask her now." Jack stood. "Are you available this evening if she says yes?"

"Sorry. Not this evening." She almost relented under the power of his gaze, but tonight was her regular shift at the soup kitchen, where she hoped against hope to find Kevin. She rose and mentally reviewed her weekend plans. Cara's birthday party was tomorrow at noon. Eileen's shower started at seven-thirty. If she stayed up late tonight and knocked out those recredentialing applications, and hit the mall for a baby gift when the doors opened, she could squeeze a trip to the hospital in between the two parties.

"If she says yes, call me in the morning and let me know. I have some time in the afternoon."

"How can I reach you?"

Becca crossed the room to her desk, wrote her cell number on the back of a business card, and turned to hand it to him. His fingers brushed hers as he took it, and again the simple contact set off a shiver of response in her. In too many ways to count, this was bad.

****

Dear God. Jack sat in his Jeep Cherokee and scrubbed his face with one hand. To say that Rebecca Bennett wasn't what he'd expected was the understatement of the millennium. He'd been sucker punched at the sight of her. Black hair cascading almost to her waist in a tumble of curls. Eyes like melting dark chocolate. In and out in all the right places. Following her down the hallway, he'd been mesmerized by the swing of her hair and the matching sway of her hips.

Definitely not a granny.

Disgruntled, he put the truck into gear with an impatient flick of his wrist. He didn't need any distractions. Head back in the game. He had a killer to stop.

****

As soon as Jack Conroy left, Becca shoved the remaining paperwork into her briefcase, pulled on her coat, and headed out. When she entered the waiting room, Denise burst into an off key song, something about a hunk-a, hunk-a burning love. Becca rolled her eyes and kept going, although she really couldn't blame Denise on this one. Jack Conroy was the most ruggedly masculine man she'd ever met. Women all over town were probably having rich fantasies about the detective that revolved around the hunk-a, hunk-a burning love concept. Halfway to her car she realized that the temperature had warmed dramatically during the afternoon and most of the snow and ice had melted.

Inside her Civic, she switched on the radio to listen to the weather and traffic report. The forecast cheered her: fifty-one degrees right now, dropping into the low forties during the night, sunny and a high of fifty-eight tomorrow. The knowledge that none of the street people, including Kevin, would freeze to death tonight lightened her heart.

She found a parking space just around the corner from the old church that housed the soup kitchen and slipped into it. When she entered a side door to the brick building, the aroma of vegetable beef stew and baking cookies greeted her. She walked down the hall, through the fellowship room, and into the kitchen.

"Hey, Becca. How's it going?" Tom Petrie greeted her with a big smile and dropped an armload of plastic trays onto the end of the counter.

"Going okay," Becca answered. "And you?"

"Can't complain."

She waved at Joe, who was setting up tables and chairs. He'd been a volunteer almost as long as she had, but she knew him the least well because he was so quiet. He was friendly, though, in a shy kind of way, and waved back before he ducked his head and turned to grab another stack of folding chairs. As far as she knew, none of the other volunteers knew him any better than she did. Once Kevin was safe and sound, she'd make a little effort to draw him out. He seemed nice enough and was better than average in the looks department, but somehow she had the feeling that he was lonely.

"Smells wonderful." Becca passed Millie Petrie, Tom's wife of forty-three years, on her way into the back room to stash her purse and coat. Millie made all the soups and stews served up to the homeless at St. Cecilia's.

Two high school girls, Ashley and Erin, were dropping chocolate chip cookie dough onto oversized cookie sheets. Heads together, they giggled and rolled their eyes when twenty-six-year-old Jeremy walked by them carrying a canister of silverware in each hand and a ream of paper napkins wedged under one arm.

Jeremy, oblivious to the girls' stares, whistled

softly as he set the spoons and napkins on the counter next to the plastic trays.

"Hot," Ashley mouthed to her friend.

Becca suppressed a grin and retrieved two large packages of sliced bologna and a jar of mayonnaise from the industrial size refrigerator. She snagged several loaves of bread and a knife, carried it all to her work station and began to assemble the sandwiches.

"Looking good, girl," Jeremy said, giving her hair a yank. "Got yourself a hell of a hairdresser."

"That I do," she answered with a smile. "And how is Todd?" Jeremy and Todd had been together for three years.

"Going crazy getting ready for the art show next weekend. He's been in a framing frenzy the last two days. You coming?"

"Wouldn't miss it," Becca assured him.

Twenty minutes later, Becca finished the first thirty sandwiches and started in on the next batch. While she worked, she kept an eye on the long line of homeless, mostly men, as they filed their way down the counter collecting a bowl of stew, a sandwich, a cup of coffee, and two cookies each. She didn't really expect to see her brother, but she couldn't stop herself from looking for him.

She spoke to Pete, an old alcoholic, and Bud, an open-faced, mildly retarded young man. A little bit later she waved at Alice, a schizophrenic woman who pushed a shopping cart containing all of her possessions ahead of her as she went through the line. Becca sighed and sent up a prayer that Kevin would not end up like Alice.

By seven twenty, the flood had thinned to a trickle.

She still had not spotted the one face she longed to see. She returned the bologna and the jar of mayonnaise to the refrigerator. As she turned back to wrap the leftover sandwiches, she automatically glanced at the door, and there he stood.

Their gazes held, and Becca started toward him. Kevin held up a hand as if to halt her approach, then whirled and ran from the room.

"Kevin," she called, but he didn't stop. Becca plunged through the thinning crowd, down the hall, and out onto the empty sidewalk.

Kevin was gone, disappeared into the night as if she'd dreamed him.

****

From underneath a parked car down the street, Kevin watched Becca as she scanned the area looking for him and battled the urge to call out to her.

He'd been broadcasting again and hadn't even known it. How else would she have found him? He gripped his head with both hands to contain the thoughts that were trying to spill out, and then shook his head rapidly back and forth, up and down, and side to side in a changing pattern so just in case some thoughts got loose they wouldn't transmit in a straight line.

The next time he looked, she wasn't there. He released a sigh of relief. He'd wanted so bad to go to her. To wrap his arms around her and feel safe. But it wouldn't be fair to her.

"It's not always about you, Kevin. Everything is not about you." Dr. Jill had said that to him once, a long time ago, and she was right. This wasn't about him. It wasn't about Becca, either. It was about Cara. About keeping Cara safe from the evil that stalked her father.

How much longer before he could see his precious little girl? He tried to remember how long he'd been gone. He'd left the last day of December. He knew that for sure, because his birthday was January first and his birthday started the countdown.

Was it April yet? It had felt like spring today. He thought it might be April. He hoped it was April. He had to stay away for a whole year. He couldn't go anywhere near Cara until his next birthday. He didn't know if he could last that long without her. Maybe he could go to her school tomorrow and watch her go down the slide from the other side of the chain link fence.

No! He banged his head against the pavement to knock that thought right out of his head. The devil had a hold of him to give him such a thought. He wrestled with the devil day and night. Like Jacob, except Jacob only had to last one night, and he had three hundred and sixty-five of them. Three hundred and sixty-five minus however many he had behind him. He wished he knew if it was April.

When he made it through the year and emerged victorious, he was going to change his name to Jacob.

****

Saturday, February 4th

Becca shut off the shower and wrapped herself in a towel, finger combed her wet hair, and slicked on some sheer lip gloss. She moved to the closet and studied its contents. The combination of lemonade and hot dogs loaded with mustard and relish, followed by birthday cake, called for casual. Disposable would be even better. She grinned at the thought of all the spills and sticky fingers in her immediate future. She grabbed a pair of jeans and a blue and green plaid flannel shirt and carried them to the bed.

Her cell phone chirped, and her lighthearted mood evaporated. She knew without looking who it was.

"Hello."

"Jack Conroy here. Juliet Crouch is agreeable to a visit from you. What time this afternoon can you see her?"

Her stomach did a nervous twist, and goose bumps popped out on her arms. The sound of his voice conjured up an image of piercing blue eyes, sharp with intelligence, and an unsmiling mouth. He wasn't the kind of man with whom a rational person wanted to play cat and mouse. She shivered.

"I can be there at three. What's her room number?"

"I'll meet you outside the gift shop at five before and take you up."

"That's not necessary. I'd rather see her alone." She realized she was speaking into dead air. He'd already disconnected.

What was she getting herself into?

****

Becca arrived at her parents' home shortly before noon. From the sounds of things, the party was already in full swing. Even with the car windows rolled up, she could hear squeals of laughter mingled with the dog's high yips.

"Aunt Becca!" She'd barely stepped inside the house when Cara, a blur of pink, launched herself into her arms. Becca gave her niece a kiss on the cheek and a quick squeeze before Cara wriggled free.

The instant her feet touched the floor, Cara raced

back to the crowd of little girls gathered around Hooligan. They took turns yelling, "Shake," and erupted into shrieks of delight when the collie lifted his paw in response.

Becca spied her stepfather affixing a cardboard donkey to the wall with thumbtacks. He grinned and waved at her. Becca grinned back at him.

"Hi, Mom," she said as she entered the kitchen. "What can I do to help?"

Marie Bennett turned and gave her a quick smile. "Hi, sweetie." Her gaze traveled past Becca, and her smile dimmed. Becca knew she'd hoped to see Kevin standing behind her.

"You're sure it was Kevin last night?"

"I'm sure."

"And he looked okay?"

"He looked fine," Becca lied.

"Okay, then. We can be grateful for that." She tried for another smile and couldn't manage it, sighed, and slumped against the countertop, wilting like a flower too long without water. "It's not safe out on the streets." She blinked rapidly as her eyes filled with tears. "I just want him to come home where he's safe."

"Me, too," Becca said softly, "but today is Cara's birthday. We need to stay focused on the party. Come on, I'll help."

"You're right." Her mother straightened her shoulders. "You pour the lemonade. I'll get these candles in the cake."

A skinny little blonde girl with pigtails won pin-the-tail-on-the-donkey. The hot dogs and chips disappeared with stunning speed.

Cara, dark eyes glowing, watched Marie light the

candles and giggled while everyone sang "Happy Birthday" to her. After the song, she closed her eyes, crossed her fingers, and made a silent wish. While her friends cheered her on, she blew out all the candles on the cake.

Cara looked expectantly at the front door, and Becca knew she'd wished for her father's return. Becca turned to her mother and saw that she, too, was eagerly watching the door. Becca realized that she herself was half expecting Kevin to make an appearance and shook her head in annoyance. If she could get her hands on her brother right now, she'd cheerfully throttle him. Everyone needed a father, but Cara more than most. Her mother had been clean and sober when Kevin met her, but she'd relapsed a few weeks after giving birth, and no one had seen or heard from her since.

A shadow of disappointment crossed Cara's face before she turned back to the table. The girls devoured their pieces of cake in record time and resumed chasing each other around the house and inciting Hooligan to nonstop barking.

Charles stood and let out a piercing whistle. "And now for the presents," he announced into the sudden quiet.

Cara unwrapped packages that contained barrettes and bracelets, neon shoelaces and CDs, a panda beanie baby, and a box of pickup sticks. She screamed when she saw the red cowboy boots from Becca and immediately dropped to the floor, pulled off her pink sneakers, and shoved her feet into the boots. She stood and began galloping around the living room. Hooligan ran alongside her, barking excitedly, and the other girls joined in, whooping and neighing and pawing at the air like rearing horses.

Standing between her parents, an arm around each of them, Becca gazed at her niece. Cara looked and acted so much like Kevin it hurt just to watch her. Becca wondered, not for the first time, if Cara had inherited more from her father than a strong physical resemblance and an outgoing personality. She desperately hoped not. The symptoms of schizophrenia hadn't manifested in Kevin until he was nineteen years old. At twenty-eight, she'd only recently quit worrying that she'd develop the disorder herself. The thought of watching Cara deteriorate and fall into the frightening, shadowy world of schizophrenia was almost unbearable.

Tears stung her eyes as she wondered again where her brother was. "Come home, Kevin," she willed silently.

****

Becca spotted Jack Conroy leaning against the wall outside the gift shop, one denim-clad leg bent at the knee and his arms crossed over his chest. His relaxed pose contrasted sharply with his continuous visual sweeping of the area. His gaze swung her way and fixed on her with all the intensity of a lion crouched in the grass, its muscles coiled to spring on the unsuspecting gazelle locked in its sights.

Becca shivered and took in a deep breath, forced her feet to keep walking toward him, when what she wanted to do was bolt and run, seek the safety of the herd.

He pushed away from the wall with casual grace, and she came to a stop. He stood a full foot taller than she. To look him in the eye she had to tilt her head so far back it put her slightly off balance.

"We're going this way." He wrapped long, blunt fingers around her arm, just above her elbow. Heat from his hand penetrated her flannel shirt and shot straight to her stomach, which tightened in response. His grasp was firm and oddly gentle as he steered her down the corridor and around a corner, past the bank of elevators, and down another corridor. She felt his touch all the way to the soles of her feet. He led with his right shoulder, his body slightly angled toward hers, and although he touched only her elbow she felt surrounded by him.

They entered a stairwell and climbed several flights of stairs. Becca was huffing for air by the time he shoved through a door and into the hallway outside the ICU. A quick look told her that his breathing remained slow and even.

"Where's...the...fire?" she gasped.

"What?" He cocked his head and raised one eyebrow.

"Give...me...a...minute." Holy Mother, she needed to get back to the gym.

"You wait here," she said when she'd caught her breath.

"I'm coming in with you."

"No, you're not." Clearly, he was used to being in charge, to getting his way. Too bad. Their staring contest ended in a draw.

"Fine," he bit out. "We'll do it your way."

"Yes," she said. "We will."

"Leave the door open then, so I can hear."

"If it's okay with Juliet."

****

It must have been okay with Juliet, as the door stayed open. Not that it was doing him any good. Jack couldn't hear a thing. Damn, but the woman had a lot of stubborn packed into her small frame. She'd challenged him and won without even breaking a sweat, a fact that filled him with equal parts admiration and annoyance.

He edged a shoulder closer to the door and peered around the frame. Okay, that explained it. There was nothing to hear. Neither one of them was talking. Becca sat in a chair beside the bed, her attention focused wholly on Juliet Crouch. Juliet lay rigid as rebar, shoulders hunched and hands fisted, staring sightlessly at the bumps her knees made under the sheet.

Well, he'd known it was a long shot. Impatiently, he drummed his fingers against his thigh. Silence continued to reign. Good God, had they both fallen asleep?

After who knew how long, he heard the murmur of voices, but he couldn't make out any of the words. He peeked again. Something was going on in that room, but damned if he could figure out what. Juliet's shoulders had relaxed, her hands were curled loosely in her lap, and her gaze now met Becca's. Neither woman was aware of him. He settled against the doorjamb to watch. Gradually his fingers stilled.

The silence, as it stretched out again, had a rich fullness to it that permeated the room and he, who could barely tolerate inaction long enough to get his required five hours of sleep a night, was content to stay right here, just like this, indefinitely, watching Rebecca Bennett work her magic on Juliet Crouch. And, indirectly, on him.

****

"She's ready to talk to you now," Becca told Jack.

"Thanks." The very edge of his mouth quirked upward in a brief almost smile, and her stomach took a slow roll. Lord help her if she was ever on the receiving end of the real thing. A full blown smile might melt her bones.

Rather than standing at the side of the bed and looming over Juliet, he sat in the chair, assuming the least threatening posture possible. If she hadn't been so flustered by his near smile, she'd have instructed him to do just that. Obviously he didn't need any coaching from her. She shouldn't have been surprised by his sensitivity to a rape victim. She knew he had two sisters; she knew what had happened to the younger one. Reminding herself that she couldn't afford to forget their shared history for a second, Becca took her post slightly behind him.

"Whenever you're ready," Jack said to Juliet. "Take your time."

Juliet drew in a deep breath and locked gazes with Becca. "He had dark eyes and eyelashes, and his eyelids were very pale."

"When he unzipped his pants, right before, ah—" She shuddered and paused, and Becca nodded encouragingly. "Right before he, ah, right before he did what he did, he said, 'Judgment Day.' "

For the first time since he'd entered the room, Juliet looked directly at Jack. Anger sparked in her eyes. "I hope you catch him, Detective Conroy."

"My personal promise to you, Miss Crouch: I'll do everything within my power to put him behind bars where he can't hurt you or anyone else ever again."

Becca had the feeling that Jack Conroy was a man

who kept his promises.

＊＊＊＊

"I'll walk you to your car," Jack said when they'd reached the first floor. He fell into step beside Becca.

"Oh, that's not necessary."

"I'll walk you to your car," he repeated, resting his hand on her shoulder. That wasn't necessary either; he just wanted to touch her.

"Fine," she said stiffly, taking a sideways step and picking up the pace. His arm fell back to his side. He hooked his thumb in his pocket to keep from reaching for her again. Clearly, she didn't want his hands on her.

"You did good work up there," he said.

"Thank you."

She was going to break into a jog any minute now.

"Where's the fire?"

She cast a startled glance at him, then laughed and slowed. He didn't remember the last time he'd teased someone, but if it earned him this kind of reward, he was going to have to do it more often.

"Need a minute to catch your breath?" she asked him with a lingering smile.

"I think maybe I do," he muttered under his breath.

"Well, here I am." She stopped beside a white Civic, unlocked the door, and slid into the driver's seat.

"Thanks for your help," he said, wishing he could think of something else to say, something that would keep her with him a little longer.

"Anytime." She waved as she drove off.

Irritated with himself, Jack watched her until she disappeared from sight. He didn't need this attraction. Didn't want it. Couldn't afford it. But he couldn't help wondering where Rebecca Bennett had been hiding all his life.

****

Sunday, February 5th

The first Sunday of every month was Mission Sunday at Church of the Lamb, and it was Georgie Burcham's favorite service. At his choosing, on a handful of other Sundays throughout the year, Pastor William called for a Mission Sunday, but always the first Sunday of every month the congregation was asked to open its heart to others in the community in need.

Georgie listened to the last note of Gloria Andrews' hymn fade away, and then watched Clara Mnich stand and walk purposefully to the podium, her long flowered skirt swirling around her legs.

"Hello," Clara said into the microphone.

"Hello," the congregation responded.

"Some of you know that I've lived with a terrible grief these past three years. By the grace of God, with the help of His servant, Pastor William, and the fellowship of this church, I have been given the strength to bear the loss of my baby girl. Brittany died of SIDS at age five months, one week, and four days." A tear rolled down her cheek, and she swiped at it with the back of her hand. Georgie's heart swelled with compassion. To lose a child, she thought, that would be the worst kind of pain.

"What none of you but Pastor William and my husband, Rob, know is that I came close to following her to the grave." A number of people shifted in the pews and murmured.

Georgie sucked in her breath as Clara's meaning came clear to her. She remembered wanting to die and trying to make it happen. She squeezed Harold's hand

and her husband of thirty-two years squeezed back. He was the only one who knew.

"Pastor told me 'Clara, that's the devil talking.' And he was right. He got down on his knees in my living room and prayed for my life and my soul. Praise God."

"Praise God," several called out.

"Praise God," Georgie whispered.

"The Lord has put it in my heart that the next step on my path to healing is service to others. We've had one offering today, and now we're going to take up another. I'm putting a hundred dollars in the plate. Everything we give right now will go to buying monitors for babies at risk for SIDS. If you're with me, say Amen."

"Amen," the people roared back at her.

Along with the majority in the congregation, Georgie Burcham opened her wallet. As she pulled out a twenty, she had a bold idea. Excitement and fear warred within her. She'd talk to Harold this afternoon and, if he supported her in this, she'd call Pastor William first thing in the morning.

****

He counted and recounted, shook his head in disbelief and counted again.

She was *old*.

He'd never done an old one. It would be nothing to subdue her. No challenge at all. She'd probably just lie there, limp and unresisting. He watched her reach for her walker and struggle to stand. A walker, for crying out loud. She wouldn't put up a fight at all.

Disappointment seeped through him at the realization. He liked it when they fought him. That was what made him hard.

Suddenly he was ashamed of himself. He was but an instrument of the Lord, who did, indeed, work in mysterious ways. Who was he to question the will of the Almighty?

He counted one last time and sighed in resignation. It was definitely the old woman.

The signs were clear.

Chapter Three

Wednesday, February 8th

He'd had to cut her first and see the blood to get hard enough to shove into her, but once he was inside her he'd been okay. All that stewing for nothing.

The fact that she lived in an independent care facility hadn't turned out to be a problem, either. In fact, it had been ridiculously easy to get to her. Oh ye of little faith, he reproached himself.

She had her own entrance. He'd even called first and set a time for her date with destiny. She'd been eager to see him. Of course, she'd thought he was delivering flowers. Women were so predictable.

Just so he'd not commit the sin of lying, he'd brought a half dozen roses. The pale, yellow petals now floated in the puddles of blood that flowed around her. Nice touch. Very nice touch. He wished he'd thought of roses for his other girls.

Unlike the one last week, this one was dead.

He'd pondered his excitement when he'd believed he'd killed Juliet Crouch and his rage when he'd learned she yet lived. He'd fasted for three days before God had revealed the answer to him. It was laughably obvious.

The wages of sin is death.

He sprinkled the remaining few petals over her.

This one was well and truly dead. Definitely and permanently dead.

This one and all who would follow.

****

Thursday, February 9th

"She didn't come to breakfast, and I thought to check on her because she was always the first one there. She liked a big breakfast, you know? She said it was from growing up on a farm, where breakfast was the most important meal of the day. So for her not to show up, it was so unusual, not like her at all, and I got to worrying. I thought maybe she'd fallen and broke her hip or something like my grandma did and was lying there waiting on someone to come find her. That happens, you know? So I said to myself, I'll just stick my head in the door, and I did, and oh, God, there she was, and all that blood, and the rose petals, oh, God, that was the creepiest thing I ever did see. I took out running as fast as I could to get Dr. Brockman. Poor thing, what her last minutes must have been like. I can't hardly stand to think about it, you know?"

Jack half listened to the young aide who had finally calmed down enough to speak coherently and give her statement to Sully, and mentally reviewed the scene in Lillian Robinson's apartment.

The door had been unlocked when the aide had checked on Lillian, so he'd made no effort to delay discovery of the body. There was no sign of forced entry. Lillian Robinson had opened the door to her killer. Had she known him?

Definitely the same perp, graduated now to murder. He'd left his signature mark above the old woman's left breast.

41

The roses were a new thing. Symbolic or merely opportunistic? Jack's guess was the latter, that he'd used the flowers to gain entrance.

Nothing about this guy added up. There was no victim profile beyond the fact that they were all women. They ranged in age from nineteen to seventy-nine. Hair color was brown, black, blonde, red, and gray. Two of them had brown eyes, two had blue, one had hazel. Andrea Marple was divorced, Nancy Rojas and Ann Wilson were married, Juliet Crouch was single, and Lillian Robinson was widowed. Four Caucasian, one Hispanic. At five foot even, Juliet Crouch was the shortest and Andrea Marple, at five ten, the tallest. They lived all over the city of Tulsa. Marple was a real estate agent, Rojas a teacher, Wilson a legal secretary, Crouch a student, Robinson the widow of a letter carrier. They were strangers to each other, and if their lives overlapped in any way, Jack hadn't uncovered that fact yet. They didn't use the same hairdresser, belong to the same health club, attend the same church, frequent the same restaurant, shop at the same grocery store, or share any other connection that he'd been able to find.

He needed to get a fix on this guy, and he needed it now. The dirt bag wasn't going to quit raping and killing on his own; someone was going to have to stop him. As hard as they'd been working on it, he and Sully were no closer to making an ID than they'd been after the first attack, five victims ago. And now Lillian Robinson was dead. How many more people would lose a mother, a wife, a daughter, a sister, while he and Sully chased their tails?

He needed facts, details, evidence, a trail to follow, damn it. He swiped a hand through his hair and swore under his breath, then stood so abruptly that his chair banged against the wall. The aide squealed and jumped. Sully raised an eyebrow. Ignoring them both, Jack strode from the room. Outside, he pulled his cell phone from his pocket and punched in Rebecca Bennett's number, tried and failed to squash the leap of anticipation swirling in his chest.

****

Even though Becca was prepared this time, the sight of Jack Conroy in her waiting room still set off a dull, clanging alarm that reverberated through her like aftershocks of an explosion. An image of him snapping on the handcuffs and reading her rights popped into her mind, and the alarm clanged louder, urging her to run. She ordered herself to get a grip—he couldn't arrest her for being Millard Harrison's daughter, for God's sake— and shoved the image firmly aside. She took a deep, calming breath, let it out slowly and drew in another.

"Detective Conroy."

"Jack," he corrected, catching her gaze and holding it as he walked across the room toward her. He advanced slowly, not stopping until he was a half step too close. She refused to back up, and she couldn't seem to pull her gaze from his.

She wished his eyes weren't such a startling shade of winter-sky blue. She really wished she didn't see the shadows of loss in their depths. Mostly, she wished she didn't know who and what had put them there.

"I've got a favor to ask. You have a minute?"

His fingertips lightly grazed her shoulder, and his deep bass rumble slid right through her. His physical nearness and the low pitch of his voice combined to create a feeling of intimacy. Her internal alarm shrieked

"Danger!" and not because she didn't feel safe with him, but because she did. He was not her friend, could never be her friend, and she'd do well to remember that the next time she had the urge to lean against his broad chest and just rest there for a minute.

"Sure." She turned, breaking eye contact and moving away from him. Even though her legs trembled, they carried her down the hallway. A minute later they were seated in her office, a safe distance apart.

Jack studied Rebecca Bennett, who eyed him warily from a few feet away. He shouldn't have crowded her. Hadn't intended to, that was for sure. He'd given himself the "she's an asset in an ongoing investigation, period" speech on the drive over. Then he'd seen her, and the speech had flown right out of his head.

He hadn't been able to resist touching her. For a few seconds, he'd thought he'd seen a softening in her posture that signaled receptivity, but then she'd stiffened and stepped back, reverted to the politely remote professional now before him—for which he ought to be profoundly thankful. His attention needed to be on catching the pervert who'd raped and murdered Lillian Robinson, not on the rich brown of Becca's eyes or the feminine sweep of her cheekbone, and certainly not on imagining the feel of all that dark, silky hair in his hands or brushing against his bare chest as—

Ruthlessly, he shut down the man in him and switched to pure cop.

"The man who put Juliet Crouch in the hospital claimed another victim last night," he stated without preamble. "Now he's progressed to murder. Latest victim was a seventy-nine-year-old widow, mother of two and grandmother of five. He filleted her like a fish."

Becca winced, but he didn't stop. He wanted to lay it all out for her, so she saw the full scope of what was at stake.

"His current pattern is one a week, for the last five weeks. Typically, we expect that interval to shorten over time. Other than the fact that they're all women, the victims appear to have nothing in common—not age, appearance, occupation, hobbies, residential areas, lifestyles, or any of the other similarities that usually form the basis of selection by serial rapists and serial killers. The investigation has hit dead end after dead end."

Now came the tricky part, the end to which he'd been building: convincing her to become a quasi-member of the investigative team. He tried to get a read on her reaction so far, but after her initial grimace her expression had remained alert, but neutral.

"What little information we have has mostly come from the women themselves. This is where you come in, I hope. Would you be willing to talk individually with the other women the way you did with Juliet Crouch?"

For a minute she didn't respond, and he thought she was going to refuse. Okay, it was a lot to ask, but he'd had to try since nothing else was panning out. Her brow furrowed. Finally, she said, "If I do, here are the ground rules: I'm a therapist first. My primary loyalty would be to the rape victims, not to the police department, and that's not negotiable."

It wasn't what Jack wanted to hear, but he reasoned they'd still get more information working with her within that limitation than they were getting without her.

"Agreed," he said reluctantly.

"I would have to be in control of my schedule," she asserted next. "I have too many responsibilities to too many people for it to be otherwise."

"Fine."

"I'm flattered that you think I can help," she said after another lengthy pause. "I need a little time to think it through. I'll have an answer for you by tomorrow afternoon."

"It would have to be on a volunteer basis," Jack added. Might as well be clear on that. The Tulsa Police Department didn't have an extra dime and wouldn't be funding any citizen consultations.

"That's not a problem for me." She looked offended at the very idea that he might have thought it would be.

He pulled a small, spiral-topped notebook and a pencil from his shirt pocket, jotted down his cell number, ripped the sheet loose and handed it to her. "Call me the minute you decide."

****

Becca mulled over Jack's request on her way to the rape-victim support group meeting that evening. Working closely with the investigation would create a perfect opportunity to position herself to advocate for Kevin if it came to that. At the same time, it would put her in close and frequent proximity to Jack Conroy, dangerous not only because she was attracted to him, but because it would keep her on his radar screen, which would increase the chances he'd discover her real identity. And if that happened, the whole thing could backfire in a big way.

While she rationalized that she wasn't lying to him, exactly, she knew he wouldn't see it that way. If it should come to light that she was the daughter of the man who'd raped and killed his eight-year-old sister, he'd be furious. She shuddered at the thought of a furious Jack Conroy. Would he take his anger out on Kevin? What else might he do if he were enraged?

She felt the remembered blow of a big man's fists and trembled, took a slow, measured breath to clear her head of that image so she could think.

Independent of her personal concerns, he was offering her a chance to help rape victims, which was the work that gave meaning to her life. She had never turned her back on a rape victim, and she wouldn't start now. If she could help the police catch the man responsible and spare even one woman, how could she live with herself if she refused to do so? Plain and simple, she couldn't. She'd call tomorrow morning and tell him yes.

****

Technically, time was up, but the newest member of the rape-victim support group had started to open up, and Becca didn't have the heart to close things down now.

"I can't get the smell of him off me," Amanda whispered. "No matter how hard I scrub, it's still there." Tears slid down her cheeks. She hunched her shoulders, ducked her head, and covered her face with raw, red hands. "I'm sorry."

"It's a terrible thing that's happened to you," Becca said, "and it's okay to cry."

Darcy passed a Kleenex to Jan, who held it out to

Amanda, who shook her head, but then took the tissue and balled it up in her fist.

"All I want is to be normal again," she whispered. "Is that too much to ask? To feel like myself again?"

"Maybe this is the new normal," Becca said, "and the new you. You've had an awful, horrifying thing happen to you, and you're not the same person you were before."

"Thank you for those words of encouragement. We are all very comforted," Dana quipped, and everyone laughed.

"You guys want to hear some good news?" Beth Ann asked. "Becca helped me remember some stuff, and I told Detective Conroy, and he caught him. Alvin Wright is the name of the man who raped me, and he is now locked up in the city jail."

The room erupted in whistles and applause and shouts of "Way to go," and "Good place for his sorry ass," and "May he rot in his cell."

"This is a good note to end on," Becca said after the noise died down.

When the group members had all left, Becca and Georgie began restoring the conference room to order.

"The kids were awful quiet tonight," Georgie commented.

"I noticed," Becca said. Neither Katy nor Shannon had said a word. "Teenagers don't stay in a primarily adult group for long. They're not comfortable, and they drop out." She sighed. "The agency needs to expand services to teens, and the board needs to figure out how to pay for it."

"I might could get us some seed money on that, if I can work up my nerve." The somber note in Georgie's voice captured Becca's full attention.

"At my church, we have mission collections on Sunday morning at the end of the service. Folks get up, say a little about themselves, talk about something they've been through personally, and witness to God's grace in their lives. Then we take up a second offering and donate that to a local service organization. Last Sunday we took up over seven thousand dollars to buy monitors for babies at risk for SIDS."

"Wow," Becca said.

"I've been talking to Pastor William. He's encouraging me to stand up this Sunday and tell about my rape." Georgie scooped up two empty foam cups from the floor and tossed them into the trash can. "If I do, how about you come lend me moral support?"

Becca hesitated. Except for Cara's baptism, she hadn't been to church in years. The first part of her life she'd prayed and begged and cried and pleaded for God to make the mean daddy go away and the nice one be there all the time. Then came Kevin's first psychotic break and subsequent diagnosis of schizophrenia, and she'd gone through the whole process over again, and with the same result. Nada. Zip. Zero.

"Well, heck, girlfriend, I'll be the one doing the hard part. All you got to do is sit on your butt and listen."

"You're right." Impulsively, Becca grasped Georgie's hand and squeezed. It wasn't going to kill her to walk through the doors of a church. "If you've got the guts to stand up in front of all those people, I'll be there."

"Thanks." Georgie's bright blue eyes filled with tears and she blinked rapidly. "You can sit with my husband, Harold. He'll make sure nobody bites you."

****

Becca had already made up her mind, so what was the point in waiting until tomorrow to inform Jack? It wasn't too late to call now; it was only a few minutes after nine.

She pulled into the lot outside of Chico's, parked the car, dug the cell phone and slip of paper he'd given her out of her purse, and punched in his number.

"Conroy."

"This is Rebecca Bennett, and I just wanted to let you know that I'll be glad to help in any way I can."

"Great. How about we meet at the Village Inn on Harvard in fifteen? I'll buy you a cup of coffee and fill you in on what we know so far. That way we can hit the ground running in the morning."

She'd been on her way downtown, to drive the streets to look for Kevin, and she'd have told him that a meeting tonight wouldn't work for her, but he'd already hung up. He'd issued an order, disguised as a suggestion, and assumed compliance. Of course, she could call him back and tell him no, which was what she wanted to do, just on general principle, but she also didn't want to get into unnecessary power struggles with him. She'd be wise to pick her battles with Jack Conroy and save her energy for the important ones.

****

Becca made it in ten and thought she might beat Jack there, but she should have known better. He was waiting at the entrance for her. Her pulse quickened in response to the intense and thorough perusal he gave her as she walked toward him.

"Appreciate your coming."

She doubted it had entered his mind that she wouldn't. She stifled the impulse to salute and simply nodded instead.

He held the door open for her with one hand and applied a slight but firm pressure at the small of her back with the other. She'd bet he was a dream dance partner, easy to follow and, good grief, why was she even thinking about dancing with Jack Conroy?

When he helped her out of her coat his hand, warm and rough, grazed the nape of her neck. Her senses leaped to life at his touch. Dangerous ground, she reminded herself, and quickly slid into the booth.

"I'm Gloria, and I'll be your server tonight." The heavyset young woman placed two glasses of water and menus on the table. "Can I bring you something to drink?"

"Coffee would be good." Jack looked at her and raised an eyebrow.

"Hot tea for me," Becca said, "with lemon."

"One coffee, one tea with lemon, coming right up." The waitress bustled off.

"I'm hungry." Jack opened the menu in front of him without looking away from her. "You hungry?"

She started to shake her head no and then caught a whiff of bacon and eggs as a waiter hurried by, realized that she hadn't eaten since breakfast, and changed the shake to a nod.

When the waitress returned, they both ordered cheeseburgers and fries.

"Hey, Gloria," a female voice from a booth behind Becca called out. "Bring me another glass of water, will you? I read about this diet where you drink a glass of water for every pound you want to lose. Weight's supposed to melt right off. I just started today, so I don't know for sure if it works or not. Wanna try it?"

"Sure." Gloria rolled her eyes. "I'll just get me a straw and head on out to Lake Keystone. First thing in the morning."

Becca laughed and glanced at Jack. A wide grin split his face and completely transformed him. Her breath caught in her throat as she got a glimpse of the boy he might have been before tragedy, in the form of Millard Harrison, had struck his family.

Her father had been on a rampage that evening, hitting walls, breaking everything he could get his hands on and arguing loudly with the voices only he could hear.

"No," he'd shouted repeatedly. "No, I won't. She's my daughter. I won't. I'm telling you, she's not part of it."

Becca had been sitting in a kitchen chair, right where he'd ordered her to sit, quiet as a church mouse, still as a statue. Kevin, who'd slipped into the room shortly after their father had made Becca come inside, sat across the table from her, eyes wide, narrow chest heaving. Suddenly, her dad had whirled toward her, snatched her off the hard chair and held her close.

"Leave her alone." Kevin had jumped from his seat and grabbed their father's arm.

Her dad had backhanded Kevin and sent him sprawling, then flung her to the floor beside Kevin, screamed at her to get out of his sight, and stormed from the house.

It was the last time she'd seen him.

"Here's your food. Can I get you anything else?"

Becca blinked and thrust the twenty-year-old

memory behind her. Both the waitress and Jack were looking at her, their faces mirroring matching expressions of concern.

"This is great. Thanks." She smiled at the waitress, picked up her cheeseburger, and turned to Jack.

"Fill me in on the other women while we eat." Her voice sounded blessedly normal. She took a bite, chewed, and swallowed.

"You okay?" Jack asked quietly.

"Just zoned out there for a minute; I'm fine. I skipped lunch, and this burger is really hitting the spot." To emphasize her words, she took another bite.

For a minute, Jack looked like he was going to challenge her, but he didn't, and she breathed a sigh of relief when he started in on his own dinner. She should have anticipated that being around him was going to trigger a lot of things for her, memories and feelings she didn't ordinarily experience.

"This guy's first known rape occurred five weeks ago," he said in between bites. "First victim was Nancy Rojas. She's twenty-eight years old, five three, brunette, brown eyes, married, has two kids ages seven and four, teaches fifth grade. Second victim was Andrea Marple, forty-four, five ten, blonde and blue, divorced, one daughter now out of the home, a Realtor. Third was Ann Wilson, thirty-four, five six, medium brown hair, light brown eyes, married, two children ages three and two months, a legal secretary. Fourth was Juliet Crouch, nineteen, five foot even, red and blue, student at TU, single, never married, no kids. Lillian Robinson was the fifth. She was seventy-nine, five five, gray and hazel, widowed, husband was a letter carrier until he retired."

He started in on his fries. Becca sipped her tea and watched his hands. He had big hands, which could have scared her but didn't. Big, strong-looking hands, with long, blunt-tipped fingers and clean, short nails. Masculine hands. Competent hands.

"All of the women report that our fella was dressed completely in black; black jeans, black sweater, black leather jacket, black gloves, black ski mask. He grabbed them all from behind. Used a knife to subdue them. Marked them all right here." He traced a pattern on the left side of his chest. "Could be the letter 't', or maybe a lopsided 'x.' " He shrugged.

"Could be a cross," Becca suggested, thinking of the Judgment Day statement that Juliet Crouch had recalled.

"Yeah." He nodded thoughtfully. "Could be a cross." He finished his fries and reached for his coffee cup. "Rojas had just the one cut, shallow. He cut Marple twice in addition to his mark, all three cuts deeper than Rojas' and all on her chest. Wilson had ten cuts in all, seven on her chest, two on her right arm, one on her face. You saw Crouch. What he did to Robinson was worse." He shook his head and glanced down, took another sip of coffee, and looked at her again.

"The evidence is good." Sharp intelligence sparked in his blue eyes as he ticked off some of that evidence. "Pubic hairs. Fibers from his clothes. Semen. Blood scraped from under Lillian Robinson's fingernails that we're pretty sure came from him; it was O positive and she was A positive. We've got enough to put him away for good once we catch him. But first we've got to catch him." He fell into a brooding silence.

"It's hard to see the ugly side of humanity day after

day, isn't it?" *What was Kevin's blood type?*

"Yeah," Jack said. "It is. Sometimes it gets to me." Crap. He couldn't believe he'd admitted that. Went against the tough cop persona he'd perfected before he'd even joined the department. Rebecca Bennett was too damn easy to talk to. There was something about the way she listened that made you feel like you could spill your guts to her and they'd land in a safe place. He sat up straight.

"Marple's schedule is pretty flexible. I thought you might start with her," he said briskly. "You have any free time in the morning?"

"My first appointment is at eight; the next appointment isn't until eleven. The two hours between nine and eleven are clear for me."

"I'll call her first thing and see if she can meet with you then."

"Just let me know."

Becca yawned, and Jack signaled for the ticket. He held her coat and surreptitiously stroked a long, dark curl as she slipped into it. The curl wrapped around his thumb and clung. Even softer than he'd imagined. He beat back the impulse to turn her around so she was facing him, plunge his fingers into all that frothy mass of hair, and hold her still while he kissed her senseless. Reluctantly, he withdrew his hands from her shoulders, pulled some money from his wallet, dropped the bills on the table atop the ticket, and shrugged into his own coat.

"I don't need any change," he told Gloria as he took Becca's arm. She didn't pull away from him or stiffen up or give him the you-are-a-lowly-cockroach look she was so damn good at, and that fact so heartened him that he moved a step nearer. She didn't react, didn't send even a subtle get-away-from-me-you-cretin signal his way. Maybe she no longer objected to his touch. Or maybe she was just getting used to it. Either way, it was progress.

Outside, as he walked her to her Honda, he dipped his head close enough to inhale the scent of her hair, a dark heavy scent that suited her and brought to mind an image of red satin sheets and candle light.

"Talk to you in the morning," she said as she slid into the Civic.

"Stay safe." He took a step back, wondering where that had come from. Those words were his standard parting caution to his sister, Courtney, a ritual begun twenty years ago, and not, otherwise, words he used. Ever.

Chapter Four

Friday, February 10th

Becca awoke to a snow covered world in which everything had been scrubbed clean, buffed to a high gloss shine, and now glistened so pure a white that it hurt her eyes. Sunlight sparkled and danced over every surface, winked at her from bushes, and glittered like fine crystal in the branches of the big oak tree in her back yard. The icicles that hung from the eaves outside her bedroom gleamed like polished silver.

She shielded her eyes with her hand and leaned closer to the glass. Her breath fogged the panes, and she wiped a spot clear with one finger. The yard beyond her duplex lay untouched, as if covered by a soft fleece blanket, smooth and unwrinkled. A thin, crusted top layer created the perfect conditions for sledding.

A picture of her first sled, cardinal red and long enough to seat two, formed clearly in her mind's eye and made her smile. She and Kevin had zoomed down the hill behind their house at breakneck speeds, over and over, dizzy with exhilaration, giddy with excitement. They'd stayed outside in the snow until their noses had been as bright as Rudolph's, until their fingers and toes had gone numb, until finally their hands and feet had felt as thick and heavy as blocks of ice. Then they'd gone inside to huddle over the floor furnace, and their mother had warmed them up with hot chocolate and snickerdoodles straight from the oven.

There'd be no hot chocolate, no floor furnace, no mother's love to warm Kevin today. The thought shattered her good mood like a rock hurled through a window. Suddenly, the snow seemed more shroud than blanket. With a shudder, she turned away from the view.

****

When Jack looked out at the snow, he saw nothing but a big inconvenience. A few inches of white stuff and the whole city shut down. Some years, Tulsa got no snow to speak of; other years—like this one—the crap was falling every damn time he turned around.

The meeting between Rebecca Bennett and Andrea Marple was probably scotched. The majority of Tulsans just stayed home in weather like this, which overall was just as well since most of them couldn't drive in snow and turned the city streets into one big bumper car arena, complete with multiple collisions and pile-ups. But the killer wasn't likely to take a vacation day, and Jack really needed something to break. He could hear the clock ticking, counting down the last remaining days and hours of the next victim.

He poured himself a second cup of coffee and punched in Rebecca's number, which he'd committed to memory at first glance and didn't need to look up.

"Hel-lo."

The sound of her voice, husky and slightly out of breath, shot straight south and immediately inspired a series of strip-the-paint-off-the-walls x-rated images that had Jack struggling to catch his breath.

"What's up?" He winced at his choice of words.

Talk about your Freudian slip.

"Scrap-ing"…pant…"my"…pant…"wind-shield. Almost"…pant…"there."

"So we're still on?"

"Yes. God bless four-wheel drive, we're still on. If Andrea Marple is willing to get out in this, I'll be there."

Jack disconnected, but the erotic pictures in his mind hadn't faded. He'd been too long without a woman, that was his problem. As soon as he could find the time, he'd call Maribel for a play date.

The thought left him flat. He didn't want Maribel. He wanted Rebecca Bennett.

****

The woman was amazing, Jack thought. All the times he'd talked with Andrea Marple and she hadn't remembered that when the rapist had taken off his right glove to unzip his pants she'd seen a gold ring glinting on his little finger. A flat, round ring with a raised letter on top. A capital B, she was positive. Even though Andrea seemed certain that the letter had been a B, Jack mentally added a capital K and a capital R to the list of potential letters, and then threw in a capital P for good measure. Of course, the letter could be either a first initial or a last, so the possibilities remained manifold. Still, it was one more puzzle piece, and the more pieces he had, the sooner they'd fit together to make a picture.

He watched Rebecca walk Andrea to the door.

"Please think about coming to group." Rebecca pressed a business card, on which she jotted down the meeting time and place, into Andrea's hand.

"I will. Thanks." The tall blonde had gone from fashionably slender to pencil thin since Jack had last seen her.

She glanced his way. Her blue eyes looked a little less haunted than they had when she'd arrived. She nodded at him, and those pale eyes darkened.

"If you think of anything else—anything at all— that I can do to help, Detective, you call me."

Andrea left, but Jack made no move to follow. The changes in Rebecca Bennett had his full attention. Gone was the woman who, until just seconds ago, had radiated calm and quiet strength. Now she fairly vibrated with tension. It had creased her forehead and pleated the skin between her eyes, pinched the corners of her full mouth. The fingers of her left hand tapped out a nervous rhythm against the palm of her right.

She swung toward her desk and began gathering up papers and files, stuffing them into her briefcase with short, jerky movements. She seemed, he didn't know what, exactly. The only word he could come up with was agitated. Clearly the work she did with rape victims took its toll. He wanted to hold her in his arms and soothe her. Instead, he cleared his throat.

She jumped and her hand came up to her throat. Then, as soon as her startled gaze settled on him, like someone had flipped a switch, her forehead smoothed out, her mouth relaxed and her fingers stilled.

"Your eleven o'clock just cancelled, Becca." The receptionist appeared in the doorway. "All of your afternoon appointments have rescheduled for next week. Is it okay with you if I close up shop and go home?"

"Good idea, Denise. Thanks for coming in. I'll see you on Monday."

"Great. As soon as I shut down the copier and the

computer, and forward the phone to the answering service, I'm out of here." Denise cut a glance toward Jack, then back at her boss, and a sly smile crossed her face. "I'll take care of everything but locking the front door. You two take your time." She winked broadly.

"Detective Conroy and I are right behind you." Becca's tone conveyed annoyance with the other woman's blatant matchmaking.

"Don't kick a gift horse in the teeth, is what I say." Denise grinned, clearly unrepentant. "Take lots of time. You may get lucky and get snowed in."

"We both have to eat lunch," Jack said after the receptionist had disappeared. "Why don't you let me treat you."

"No, thanks." She pulled on her coat, hoisted the packed briefcase in one hand, slung her purse over the other shoulder, and headed for the waiting room, leaving him to trail along in her wake. No excuses, no apologies, just a flat refusal and a foot race to the door. Okay, he could take a hint.

When he took her elbow to help her down the front steps, she flinched, and as soon as she reached flat pavement, she pulled away. So much for progress. She was back to treating him like he was a carrier of some deadly, contagious disease. He just wished he could figure out what had put her into reverse. She was a complicated woman, Rebecca Bennett was.

Unfortunately, it would seem that he'd recently developed a taste for complicated women.

****

The cold hand of dread had settled on the back of Becca's neck and wouldn't let go. Chills rippled across her shoulders and down her arms, skipped along her spine to her legs. Her hands shook, and her teeth chattered like castanets.

Kevin had a ring exactly like the one Andrea Marple had described in detail.

On the day their adoption had been finalized, Charles Bennett had taken them all out to dinner at the Warren Duck Club to celebrate. He'd presented Becca with her new initials, RB, on a thin gold chain. To Kevin, he'd given a gold signet ring with a B for Bennett. They'd both treasured those symbols of their new identities—new father, new family, new lives free from violence and fear.

She fingered the necklace that even now she wore beneath her sweater. As far as she knew, Kevin never took his ring off, though by his senior year in high school he'd had to switch it from his ring finger to his little finger. Her stomach clenched.

He wore it on his right hand.

Please, please, please let it be on his dresser, she chanted silently as she drove to her parents' home.

She took the corner at 41st and Utica too fast and fishtailed. She turned into the skid, eased off the gas, and the car straightened out. A few minutes later, she parked by the curb in front of her childhood home. A row of snow angels lined the walk to the porch; Cara had been busy this morning.

"Hello," she called out as she walked through the front door.

"In the kitchen," her mother called back. "Come join us for soup and sandwiches."

"Aunt Becca," Cara squealed, skidding around the corner of the dining room and grabbing Becca's hand. "It's gonna be really good. I chopped the carrots and onions myself."

The mere thought of food made Becca's stomach roll, but she wanted to keep things as normal as possible for Cara so she allowed herself to be pulled into the kitchen and accepted the bowl that Cara proudly set in front of her.

"Aunt Becca, did you know the first time my daddy helped make vegetable soup he cut his finger?"

"He did?"

"It was so funny." She giggled. "Tell her, Grandma."

"It wasn't even a cut, really, just a tiny, little nick, but he insisted on a big band aid." Marie smiled. "Then he went to kindergarten the next day and told his whole class that the blood spurted and spurted until he almost had to have a transfusion."

"That's Kevin: The King of Exaggeration." Becca laughed and then sobered as she remembered Jack mentioning that the killer's blood type was O positive. Her mind raced. What were the chances her mother knew Kevin's? How to find out without setting off any alarms? "Reminds me, though, to go donate soon. I heard the Red Cross is running low. I keep meaning to ask them what my blood type is; maybe this time I'll remember."

"You're O positive. Don't look so shocked, dear. I haven't developed a steel trap mind; I only know because I'm negative. Your dad was O positive and both you kids were O positive, too. I took the Rhogam shots. I was always so grateful for those shots. Otherwise I'd have lost you both."

"Do you like our soup, Aunt Becca?"

"I do." The room was spinning, and she couldn't

catch her breath. "It's delicious," she managed to choke out. She forced down two spoonfuls before she rose from the table.

"I'm headed to the Day Center for the Homeless and thought I'd grab a change of clothes for Kevin, in case he stops in there," she whispered to her mother as Cara climbed on top of the counter to grab a handful of snicker doodles out of the cookie jar.

"Good idea," Marie whispered back.

It was, and she didn't know why she hadn't thought of it before now, when she needed an excuse to go through his things and search his room. She carried a brown paper grocery sack with her into Kevin's bedroom and closed the door behind her.

The ring was not on his dresser. Not in his dresser. Not on his bedside table. Not in his room anywhere. A quick check told her it wasn't in his bathroom either.

Her stomach muscles cramped around the soup she'd forced down. The ring was with Kevin, doubtless on the little finger of his right hand.

Was history repeating itself?

The shaking started in the center of her chest and spread outward until her whole body trembled like an autumn leaf in a storm. Images of the old nightmare exploded in her mind: her father at the mercy of the voices, she and Kevin sprawled on the floor, the police with their badges and their questions, the flash of television cameras, the screaming of reporters, the mental pictures her own imagination had supplied of the bloodied, lifeless body of Megan Conroy, the private shame and the public humiliation, both fueled by her own secret knowledge, the paralyzing guilt. Her knees buckled, and she sank onto the edge of the bed.

Breathe, she ordered herself. *Breathe.* She couldn't possibly help anyone else if she didn't get a grip on herself. And if Kevin was following in their father's footsteps, her family would need her now more than ever. Her mother was a sweet and loving person but not a strong one. It would be up to Becca to hold them all together. Kevin, who was not bad, just tortured. Marie, wonderful in her own way, but weak. Charles, a good and decent man who had not known Millard Harrison and who liked to pretend that everyone's life had started the day he and Marie had gotten married. And Cara, precious Cara, the true innocent in all this.

Slowly, breath by breath, she brought herself under control.

She stuffed thermal underwear, two pairs of thick wool socks, two heavy sweatshirts, and corduroy pants into the sack and carried it all out to her car.

****

He was cold, so very cold. Was it January again? If it was January, he'd made it through the whole year, and he could go home. He really wanted to go home.

This sure felt like January, but that couldn't be right. It had been April just a few days ago. Hadn't it? He wished he had a calendar to carry in his pocket and a pencil. He could mark the days off, one at a time, with a big X, like he'd done as a kid, counting down the days until Christmas. Going home at the end of this year would be better than all of his Christmases rolled into one.

"Hey," he shouted at a woman coming out of the library. "What day is it?"

The woman ducked her head and hurried to her car.

"You, there," he yelled at her. "I'm talking to you."

She slammed her car door shut and locked it. A man coasting by in a blue Ford Explorer rolled his window down as he passed him and said, "It's Friday, buddy."

Friday? He'd left on a Saturday. Maybe he'd only been gone a week. Oh, God. Which was it? A week? Or a year? A year? Or a week? He grabbed his head and turned in circles as the sharp knife of panic slashed at him.

Time had shifted and doubled back on him. Week. Year. Week. Year. He was trapped in a time tunnel, an endless loop, and he didn't know how to get out of it.

He couldn't help himself; he started to cry. *Baby. Sissy.* He could hear his father's jeering insults, but he couldn't stop the tears. Because if he couldn't get out of the time tunnel, he'd never see his daughter again.

He swiped at the tears with the back of his hand and reminded himself that he was doing this for Cara. To keep her safe from the evil that stalked her father.

****

After she'd dropped the clothes off at the Day Center and talked to the staff—both David and Darlene reported seeing Kevin the day before, but not so far today—Becca slowly drove the streets of downtown, which were practically deserted, looking down alleys and peering between buildings, hoping against hope she'd find her brother and end this nightmare.

If his behavior last week was any indication, Kevin didn't want to come home, but if she saw him again, by golly, she'd drag him kicking and screaming if she had to, first to Dr. Maganas and then back to where he belonged—with his family.

Late afternoon shadows darkened the covered

parking area between the library and the police department. She coasted slowly, alert to any movement. As she scanned the garage, her mind spun backward.

She'd been so shaken up by Andrea Marple's detailed memory of the ring her assailant had worn that after the woman had left she'd completely forgotten that Jack Conroy was still sitting there. All she'd been able to think about was Kevin. Had she spoken his name out loud? She didn't think so. Hoped not. She'd definitely lost it, but her lapse hadn't lasted long. Maybe he hadn't noticed.

Quit kidding yourself. The man is a trained observer, for Lord's sake. And no way had he not noticed how abrupt—okay, downright rude—she'd been when he'd asked her to join him for lunch.

She sighed. It was probably for the best. Maybe Jack would quit trying to nudge things between them to a more personal level. She tightened her jaw against the pang of loss that squeezed her chest. She ought to be glad. If there was one thing she couldn't afford to do, no matter how tempting it was, it was to get up close and personal with Jack Conroy.

And speak of the devil. As if her thoughts had conjured him out of thin air, Jack pulled into a parking space outside the police department entrance and stepped out of his black Jeep. Just the sight of him made her heart beat faster. She told herself it was apprehension that made her pulse race but knew deep down that was only half of the story. Although, truly, she'd never seen a more ruggedly handsome man, that wasn't what made him so compelling.

As if he could feel her gaze on him, he glanced around the garage and saw her. He raised a hand in greeting and immediately changed direction.

He walked toward her like a man on a mission, his muscular legs eating pavement in long, purposeful strides. His shoulders looked wide enough to carry whatever needed carrying. For just an instant, she wondered what it would feel like to share her responsibilities with someone like Jack. He faced ugly realities every day, and he did not avert his gaze, or turn away, or pretend those realities didn't exist.

When he reached her, he braced a hand on the car door and leaned down. She looked up into blue eyes that focused on her with such intensity that she felt stripped bare and exposed. Had he somehow figured out who she really was? Adrenaline shot through her and produced a panicked urge to run.

"What brings you to my part of town?"

I'm looking for my brother, who may be the same man you're looking for wouldn't do. She swallowed a bubble of hysteria.

"Nothing," she said quickly. Too quickly, judging by the frown that crossed his face. The question called for a casual response, but her mind was blank as an egg shell. Nothing came to her. She settled for a shrug.

For a long moment neither of them spoke. Becca looked away first, and once she was freed from his gaze, she realized that the truth, or a portion of it, would do fine.

"I volunteer at the soup kitchen every Friday evening, which is where I'm headed now." She glanced at her watch. "I'd better scoot, or I'll be late."

He straightened and rapped the hood of her car with his knuckles. "Drive carefully. The streets are slick."

"Will do." She raised the car window, took her foot off the brakes, and eased out onto the street.

Drive carefully. Why those simple words should produce such a warm glow was beyond her, but they had. She pulled to the curb outside the church that housed the soup kitchen, still pondering her odd reaction. He'd actually seemed concerned for her safety! It struck her, as she shut off the engine, that she worried about other people's safety and well-being practically nonstop—her brother, her niece, her parents, her friends, even her clients—but rarely did that concern run the other direction. It wasn't that her family and friends didn't love her, because she knew they did. It was just that she was the strong one on whom everyone leaned, and it didn't occur to them to worry about her.

She'd had no idea it could feel so nice—weird, but nice—to have someone worry a little about her.

****

Jack wanted to kick himself all the way around the block. Was he the master of casual conversation, or what? *Drive carefully, the streets are slick?* Like she wouldn't notice that all on her own and he had to point it out to her? Just the sight of her turned him stupid. One look and his IQ dropped into the idict range.

How else to explain that he'd gone charging across the parking garage the minute he'd spotted her, in spite of the fact that she'd made it perfectly plain, just hours ago, that she wanted nothing to do with him?

It really bothered him that she'd seemed so nervous, almost like she was afraid of him. So he was no good at small talk. He hated small talk. He liked it when people got straight to the point and said what they had to say, but he couldn't just walk up to her car and ask her if she'd get naked with him. He'd had to come up with something a little more socially acceptable. And while "What brings you to my part of town?" wasn't the smoothest thing he could have said, he couldn't see why it would have spooked her, either.

He'd like to think that the same sexual awareness that had a choke hold on him was putting her off balance, but he doubted that was the case.

He reviewed the interaction again. She'd definitely acted nervous. Fearful. If she'd been a suspect, the word he'd pick would be guilty.

Guilty?

He didn't get it. Why would she want to hide the fact that she'd been at the library? Although, come to think of it, she hadn't actually said she'd been at the library, he'd merely assumed that's where she'd been. Maybe she'd been at the police station. But still, no big deal. He couldn't imagine she had anything more serious than a parking ticket or a speeding citation, which didn't account for guilty.

It didn't make sense. He was missing something. Something big.

Jaw set, he returned to his Jeep. He didn't know why she'd lie about doing volunteer work or why she'd be nervous about being caught going to the soup kitchen, but it was easy enough to check out.

****

Her cell phone chirped, and Becca welcomed the distraction from thoughts about Jack Conroy, her reactions to him, and what might be possible if circumstances were different.

"Hi, Eileen. You have that baby?"

"I wish. Carol Fox just called from Channel Two. In light of our serial rapist turned killer, she's wanting to interview someone about safety tips for women. Says it'll be a short piece, probably a thirty second spot, and they want to air it tomorrow at both six and ten. Okay if I give her your number?"

"Sure. You really owe me now."

"If it's a girl, I'll name her after you."

****

Jack pulled up to the corner, looked to his right, and spotted Becca's car parked at the curb just outside St. Cecilia's. The tension in his shoulders eased. Okay, so she really was a volunteer at the soup kitchen. It fit with what he'd observed of her.

He felt half an inch tall. The woman was exactly what she appeared to be: a kind, giving person who genuinely cared about other people. She was willing to donate her time—to rape victims, to the mentally ill, and the homeless—for no other purpose than to help, and the world could use more people like her.

He shook his head, annoyed with himself. Cynicism and suspiciousness were occupational hazards, the results of seeing the ugly side of humanity day after day, as Becca had put it. She'd been evasive—probably because she could tell that he was drawn to her and she didn't feel the same pull to him—and he'd seen guilt, deception, and cover up.

By force of habit he scanned the area. Homeless men and women were converging on the church, singly and in groups of twos and threes. Some of them he recognized on sight, including Leon, who'd been living on the streets since before Jack had joined the department, and Alice, a relative newcomer, who pushed her cart up and down the city sidewalks and had lively conversations with inanimate objects. Now she carried on an enthusiastic, if one sided, discourse with Becca's car.

As he turned the corner, he saw that Alice wasn't gesturing at the Honda after all, but at a slightly built man who knelt in the street by the driver's door. His hands covered his ears and he rocked back and forth on his knees, head swinging side to side and then up and down.

"Git," Alice shouted and waved one hand like she was shooing a cat. "Go on, git!"

The man sprang to his feet, hands still over his ears, head bobbing as he ran. He bumped Alice's cart as he went by her, sending it careening into a parking meter where it bounced and spun out into the street.

Jack swerved to the curb and slammed the Jeep into park, jumped out, and seized the runaway cart. He pushed it toward Alice, who backed away from him.

"No trouble," she said, hands up in the surrender position. "Don't want no trouble, Mr. Detective."

"You're not in trouble, Alice." He maneuvered the cart over the curb and onto the sidewalk, and then took a few backward steps.

Alice grabbed the cart and pushed it in the same direction the homeless man had gone, shaking her head and muttering, "No trouble, Mr. Detective, Alice don't want no trouble."

Jack turned and headed back to his Jeep. He ought to have compassion for the mentally ill, but he didn't. He'd read up on schizophrenia and knew it was a bio-chemically based thought disorder that afflicted approximately one percent of the population. He knew that the majority of those who suffered with it, who were tormented by it, were harmless.

But Millard Harrison had been a paranoid schizophrenic, and the man who'd raped and murdered Megan sure as hell hadn't been harmless.

Passing Becca's car, his gaze fell on a triangle of thick brown paper wedged under the rubber strip around the driver's side window. He stopped and leaned down to examine what appeared to be part of a grocery sack. The tiny cramped words on it had been written in pencil with enough pressure to tear the paper in several places.

Stay away, B. Not safe. The year of evil has begun. I am fighting demon spirits daily. Pray 4 victory. Love, K. P.S. Thankx 4 the clothes. P.P.S. Stay away and I mean it.

Chapter Five

Friday, February 10th

Stay away and I mean it. Concerned warning? Or camouflaged threat? Did Becca know the head bobbing, homeless man? He'd addressed her by the first initial of her name. And signed off with Love, K., and that indicated a personal relationship. Then again, maybe the personal relationship was all in his imagination. Maybe the homeless man had noticed her one Friday evening as he'd gone through the soup line and become fixated on her. No question about it, the head bobber was seriously whacked. Was Becca in danger? Directly from the homeless man himself? Just in his delusions? Or, as the note implied, from elsewhere? Not from free floating demon spirits—Jack didn't believe in those. The only demon spirits Jack believed in were the living, breathing ones who inhabited human bodies, like Millard Harrison.

The pairing of Becca and Millard Harrison in the same thought turned his blood to ice. Just the idea of a monster like Millard Harrison being obsessed with Becca covered him in a cold, clammy sweat.

He made his way back to the Jeep and considered his options. He had to assess the threat to Becca, and to do so he had to discuss the note with her. How to explain how he'd happened to be there and to read the note in the first place without coming across as a stalker himself? Too many questions and not enough answers. Story of his life.

****

Dispirited, Becca buttoned her coat, fished the car keys from her purse, and said her goodbyes to the other volunteers. She hugged Jeremy, waved at Tom and Millie Petrie, and spoke to Joe, who surprised her by answering with, "Take care of yourself. It's bad out there," instead of giving her his usual nod. Although the soup line had been long and St. Cecilia's Fellowship Hall full to overflowing, she'd not seen the one face she longed to see.

Freezing winds lashed her when she stepped outside. She struggled to keep her footing as she navigated the ice-covered pavement and wondered where Kevin would sleep on this frigid night. Tears filled her eyes as she slipped and slid her way to the car. Blinking back the hot tears, she unlocked the door.

A heavy footstep sounded behind her, followed by a muffled oath. She looked over her shoulder in time to see Jack Conroy's feet go out from under him. He made a wild grab for the back bumper of her Honda, missed, and landed hard on his backside.

When he tried to stand, his feet slipped again, and he went back down. This time there was nothing muffled about the oath.

"Damn it to hell." He lay sprawled beside her rear tire, spotlighted by the street light.

"Are you okay?" Becca clung to the open car door, turned toward him and took a half step, slid, and stopped where she was.

"Dandy," he said, carefully picking himself up.

"Just damn dandy." This time he remained upright.

Becca choked back a giggle as he lurched his way toward her. In a black leather coat and white muffler, stumbling side to side, flatfooted on the ice, he brought to mind the image of a drunk penguin.

"Go ahead and yuk it up." He cast a wry grin her way. "I live to amuse."

"And doing a fine job of it, too." She couldn't help herself, the laughter she'd been holding in burst loose when he skated into the side of the car, arms flailing and knees wobbling. He managed to steady himself on the roof of the car, or he'd have hit the ground again.

She almost had her laughter under control, and then the instant replay flashed in her mind, and she saw it all over again. This time she laughed so hard she doubled over with it, lost her grip on the car door, and almost went splat herself.

"I've got you." He snaked out a hand and caught her elbow. She grabbed his other arm. The next thing she knew they were doing an awkward waltz on the ice, holding on to each other and fighting to stay on their feet. By the time they came to rest against the open car door, his grin stretched from ear to ear.

Becca looked up into sparkling blue eyes and smiled. Gradually the mirth in his eyes was replaced by something much more heated. The intensity in his gaze stole her breath, and something she couldn't name sprang to life inside her, hummed just beneath her skin until she was dizzy with it. The world dropped away, and there was only the strength of his arms, the warmth of his breath on her face, the promise in his eyes as his head dipped closer.

"Night, Becca." Tom Petrie's voice penetrated the

haze that surrounded her and broke the spell.

"Night, Tom," she called back, surprised that she could sound so normal when she could barely breathe. "See you next week."

Thank heavens Tom had come by and interrupted when he had, or she'd be kissing Jack Conroy right now. The last man on the planet she needed to be kissing, and unfortunately the only one she wanted. Life was a cruel teacher, but she was an apt student, and if there was one lesson she'd learned well, it was that she couldn't always have what she wanted, no matter how badly she wanted it.

Wedged between Jack and the car door, she couldn't move. She cleared her throat. Jack took a step back, and she was again aware of the penetrating cold.

"I need to talk with you about the message on your car."

"What message? Where?"

"There." He gestured behind her. "I'll get it." He reached around her, briefly cocooning her in his warmth, and pulled a scrap of paper from the window and handed it to her.

She recognized her brother's handwriting immediately. "Kevin," she breathed as she slid into the driver's seat and turned on the interior car light. She scanned the note quickly and then read the words again, slowly. Unchecked by medication, the full force of paranoia had been loosed upon him. As was so common with schizophrenia, the delusions wore the disguise of religious revelations. She pictured him, wild eyed and terrified, flapping his hands or covering his ears as he did when the voices held sway, and her heart broke.

"Who is Kevin?" Jack asked.

She'd forgotten he was there. Her mind scrambled for the right words to cover her slip and came up empty. She shivered under the onslaught of an icy wind, and the hopelessness of the last six weeks washed over her.

In spite of her best efforts, her brother was still out there all alone, wrestling demons only he could see and hear. She knew Kevin was afraid of the dark—they both were—and yet he was out there, lost in a darkness deeper than night, trapped in an inner cold more profound than the current arctic temperature. If he froze to death tonight, would she console herself that she'd protected his identity?

Hope blossomed as it occurred to her that Jack could help her find Kevin without ever knowing who it was he'd found.

"My brother," she said, quickly, before she could change her mind. "He's mentally ill. He hears voices and disappears when he doesn't take his medicine." She ignored the brief flash of distaste on Jack's face; she knew where it came from, who he was thinking about. "I've been trying to find him so I can get him to his doctor and back on his meds, but he's hiding from me." She was mortified by the flood of tears that rolled down her cheeks, and futilely tried to stop the flow. When she couldn't, she averted her face.

"Get me a picture of him, and I'll put the word out to the guys on patrol. We'll find him."

"Thank you." She swiped at her cheeks with the back of her hand.

"Look at me, Becca." Jack leaned down and, with a finger under her chin, tipped her face up. He smoothed away her tears with his thumb. "We'll find him."

****

So her brother was mentally ill. That was probably what had motivated her to become a therapist. And a damn good one, as he had reason to know and appreciate. He knew how that worked. Hadn't he been driven to become a cop because of what had happened to Megan? And wasn't he good at his job for the same reason she was good at hers? Because it was personal. Because it was a chance to right old wrongs, maybe spare someone else the pain you had to live with every day, fix for someone else what you couldn't fix for yourself.

He'd find Becca's brother. Whatever he had to do, whatever it took. Starting now. His sister was lost to him forever, but he'd bring her brother back to her, alive if not well.

He and Rebecca Bennett had more in common than she could possibly know.

****

Saturday, February 11

"Here's a picture of Kevin." Becca handed the photograph to Jack. She'd deliberately chosen the picture she'd snapped right after he'd come home the last time, before he'd had a chance to shave or get a haircut or get cleaned up. She'd wanted to show Kevin how low he sank when he quit his meds and took off. That picture had been taken two years ago last summer. Obviously, he hadn't gotten the message, but she imagined he looked much the same now, with the addition of a hat and heavy coat.

"I'll make some copies and get them to the guys on patrol." Jack slipped the picture into his shirt pocket.

Becca flipped the lights on in the waiting room and headed directly for the kitchen to start the coffee. She'd

79

arrived at her office early, but Jack had already parked and was waiting when she pulled in. Nancy Rojas was supposed to be there at nine o'clock; fifteen minutes from now. What were she and Jack going to talk about for fifteen minutes? Not Kevin, if she could help it. She'd answered every question Jack had asked her last night about Kevin's habits, where he'd gone in times past, who he knew, how he perceived things.

She'd begun having second thoughts the minute she'd driven away. She kept repeating silently that no good could come from second guessing herself now. It had felt right at the time. What was done was done. She'd tossed the dice, and all that was left was to hope for the best possible outcome.

She scooped coffee grounds into the filter and moved to the sink to fill the carafe with water. Jack got three mugs out of the cabinet and set them on the countertop. His arm brushed hers, and the contact was oddly comforting. She lingered there, soothed by the physical connection.

"Weatherman says we'll hit upper forties today and get sunshine this afternoon. Supposed to melt most of the snow and ice before tonight."

"That's good news." She knew he was thinking about her fears for Kevin and was trying to reassure her. The tightness in her chest eased. Asking him for help had been the right thing to do.

She filled two mugs with coffee and handed one of them to him. They stood side by side, sipping coffee and gazing out the window in companionable silence. A pair of cardinals ate sunflower seeds that she'd put out after the first deep frost; a circle of empty shells lay on the snow covered ground beneath them. With Jack's help, Kevin would be in out of the cold soon, maybe even today, before the sun could melt the snow and ice. Gratitude welled in her chest. It felt so good to share a part of her burden with someone else, to draw strength from his reassurance and competence, even if that someone else could never know her real identity or that of the man whose picture rested in his coat pocket.

Oh, how she wished he were anyone other than the man whose sister had died at her father's hand. But wishing things to be different than they were was an exercise in futility; that was another lesson she'd learned at a very young age. How many times had she wished that her daddy wouldn't get so mad? That he'd stop hitting? That the voices would go away and leave him alone? And after, that he'd never left the house that night? That Megan Conroy hadn't been outside that evening? She turned away from Jack to busy herself with wiping an already clean countertop.

Jack stared at the back of Becca's head, perplexed by the sudden shift in her mood. He'd like to know what had triggered the brief smile that had lit up her face just seconds ago, and he'd give anything to understand what had doused it. The silence that had been companionable was now strained. Damned if he could figure out what had caused her mercurial change. She'd seemed almost relaxed, and now she was about to scrub the finish off the Formica countertop. He raked his fingers through his hair and swallowed a sigh of frustration. It was one step forward, one step back; he hadn't made any net progress at all toward his goal of gaining Rebecca Bennett's trust and making her feel comfortable with him. Should he ask or let it go?

The creak of the front door opening interrupted his

internal debate. Nancy Rojas had arrived.

He made it to the waiting room before the petite Hispanic woman had closed the door behind her. Becca was right on his heels. He introduced the two women and offered Rojas a cup of coffee, which she refused, holding up her travel mug by way of explanation.

The three of them adjourned to Becca's private office. Once they were seated, Becca fixed her attention on Rojas so completely that Jack imagined a bomb blast wouldn't register with her. He'd never seen anything quite like the total concentration and in-the-moment, fully-present attentiveness that Becca brought to her work. He'd been accused of being as aggressive as a pit bull when he was digging for information, but Becca's concentration was altogether different, more like a calm, deep lake in which a person could float, fully supported, and release their secrets into her safekeeping.

How did she do that? Convey without a word that there was no thought too dark and no feeling too disturbing, no shadow too sinister to safely share with her. Even as an outsider, a mere observer, Jack again felt the same mysterious peace he'd experienced outside Juliet Crouch's hospital room steal over him, seep into him, soothe him. His body relaxed into the chair. The fingers he'd been impatiently tapping against his thigh stilled. His jaw loosened. Something in his chest eased.

The soft silence began to swell and ripen into something strong and solid enough to bear the weight of words heavy with memories and meanings.

Haltingly at first, gaze locked onto Becca's, Nancy Rojas began to recount her experience with the man who'd raped her, how he'd grabbed her from behind off her own front porch and wrestled her into the bushes along the front of her house, held the knife to her throat and threatened her children, inside with a teenage babysitter, if she made a sound. Her fingertips traced the shape of the mark he'd cut into the fleshy upper slope of her left breast.

" 'Judgment Day, Mary.' That's what he said when he did this." Her fingers outlined the mark again, down and then across. " 'Judgment Day, Mary.' "

****

"Looked to me like she was making the sign of the cross," Jack said after Nancy Rojas had gone.

"Looked that way to me, too." Becca nodded in agreement. "It fits with the other religious references. Judgment Day. Mary, the mother of Christ."

"So what variety of nuts is our guy?" He regretted his choice of words the second they were out of his mouth. She'd confided in him about her missing brother who heard voices, and he popped off about "nuts." *Way to go, Conroy*, he congratulated himself at the stiffening of her shoulders. "Sorry," he added quickly. "That didn't come out right."

"Don't worry about it." She straightened and slid the legal pad on which she'd jotted notes into her briefcase and then shrugged into her coat.

He wanted to kick himself. With a few careless words, he'd destroyed their fragile connection. The woman who'd stood next to him in the kitchen an hour and a half ago, sipping coffee and watching the cardinals just outside the window, had withdrawn from him as completely as if she'd removed herself to another planet.

"Sorry," he repeated.

"No apology necessary," she said crisply. With a slight nod of her head, she slipped into polite professional mode. "It's impossible to make a diagnosis based on the little information I have. He appears to be suffering delusions of a religious nature. Psychotic features are associated with a variety of disorders."

He hated the smooth, impersonal tone, the guarded set of her shoulders, the coolness in her eyes. One step forward, three steps back this time, and all his own doing. *Focus on the case*, he ordered himself.

"Any tentative conclusions, or even just speculation, about the subject that you can make at this time?"

"I would guess that he's in and out of psychosis because he's highly organized. There's nothing impulsive about his attacks. He plans them. He prepares. He brings a knife with him. He probably functions fairly well in some areas of his life. Work, for example, where he likely performs repetitive, standardized duties, the same sequence of actions over and over with little variation." She picked up the briefcase with her left hand and the now empty coffee mug with her right, and walked briskly to the kitchen, leaving him to follow along behind her.

"His job wouldn't require him to interact with people except briefly," she continued. She set the mug in the sink and flipped the coffee pot switch to the off position. "I imagine that his relationships would be primarily superficial, and the few that aren't surface only would be intense and highly volatile." She turned around to face him. "Goes without saying that he was abused as a young child."

"And why does that go without saying?" he asked, keeping the sneer out of his voice when what he really wanted to do was roll his eyes. He'd always thought that one was pretty lame and just a way to excuse the awful things people did. Her lips thinned, so maybe he hadn't stifled the sneer after all.

"Because the human brain isn't fully differentiated until age five or so, and the area of the brain that controls aggression is adjacent to the area of the brain that governs sexuality. When a child is abused, it triggers aggression even if it's not safe to act on it, and some of those electrical charges are firing into the part of the brain that relates to sexuality. If this happens enough, a link between violence and sexuality is established. The most often physically abused child is male. That's why." The bite in her voice made it clear that he'd annoyed her.

"You may have missed your calling as a profiler," he commented, impressed by her knowledge and observations.

She tilted her head, sending a nod of acknowledgment his direction, but offered no comment, and made her way to the door, turning off lights as she went.

"I'm headed to the Full Moon for lunch. If you'd like to join me, that'd be great," he offered, knowing as he did so that she'd refuse, thanks to his big mouth.

"Thanks, but I have errands and an appointment."

"Okay, then. I'll meet you back here at two for the interview with Ann Wilson," he said, as she locked the door behind them.

"Two," she agreed.

****

The interview with Carol Fox had gone well. The petite blonde reporter had put Becca so at ease that she'd forgotten the camera. Becca had issued the standard precautions and safety tips: be aware of your surroundings; don't go off alone, stay with a group; carry your cell phone and pepper spray; if you think someone is following you, call the police; never go willingly to a more isolated place; verify the identity of the person on the other side before opening your door; check the back seat before getting into your car; lock your car doors; be extra vigilant when getting into and out of your car, and entering or leaving your home, as those were the times of greatest vulnerability. She hoped that women of all ages in Tulsa would heed the warning, and knew that most would not. The majority of people assumed that bad things always happened to someone else. Channel Two News would run the spot during the six and ten o'clock broadcasts tonight.

Back in her car, Becca checked the time: a little before one. She decided to swing by Wendy's, pick up a salad, and take it with her to her office. She'd eat at her desk and jot down her notes on the session with Nancy Rojas. As she pulled out onto Twenty-First Street, she noticed that the sun had indeed come out. The roads were almost clear, and here and there patches of grass showed through the rapidly melting snow. Jack had been right.

At the thought of Jack, her stomach clenched. He thought he'd offended her with his use of the word "nuts," but what had really brought her up short was the reminder, which evidently she needed repeatedly, that she couldn't let down her guard for a minute, couldn't assume understanding, let alone empathy, from him when it came to Kevin. He'd help her find her brother, she had no doubt about that, but if Kevin were responsible for the string of sexual assaults, his mental illness would induce displaced revenge, not compassion, in Jack. Not that she could blame him.

Well, she'd cross that bridge when she came to it. If she came to it. And that "if" was a big "if." The voices Kevin heard had urged him to do strange and bizarre things, but as far as she knew, the voices her brother heard had never demanded violence the way their father's voices had. So the likelihood that he'd suddenly turned serial rapist, or murderer, was slim. Wasn't it? Except she knew what he'd been subjected to, and what he'd witnessed. She knew the images that rolled around in his head; she had the same images in hers. She knew his worst nightmare; they'd lived it together. And every day, in her line of work, she saw history repeating itself. She saw women who'd been beaten as children choose abusive partners. She saw men who had watched their fathers hit their mothers use their fists on their wives. She mapped out families of origin with every new client and traced the patterns of alcoholism and drug addiction, physical and sexual abuse, and mental illnesses back three and four generations. What wasn't fixed in one generation got passed down to the next.

"Stop it," she ordered herself out loud as she unlocked the office door and stepped inside. "Just stop it." She was engaging in what Eileen laughingly referred to as "high speed circular thinking," and it would get her nowhere except, as Jack had so eloquently put it, nuts.

And now her thoughts had circled back around to

Jack. That was another track that would get her nowhere. She set the salad on her desk with a thump and slipped out of her coat. She had to quit thinking about Jack Conroy. She especially had to quit reliving that near kiss last night. One almost kiss had scrambled her brains and loosened her tongue. If she were an alcoholic wanting to drink with the same intensity she wanted do-overs on that almost kiss, she'd be calling her sponsor right now. Because, while her head knew that personal involvement with him would be disaster, her heart and her hormones couldn't seem to get the message. She was walking a tightrope with no safety net to catch her if she fell. If she lost her balance, she wouldn't be the only one to get hurt. Her whole family would suffer the consequences.

****

The raised scar that ran from Ann Wilson's right cheekbone to the corner of her mouth lay on her face like a dark pinkish purple strand of wet spaghetti. While her flesh was repairing itself, the damage to her spirit hadn't even begun to heal. She clutched her husband's hand like it was a lifeline, gripping so tightly that her knuckles stood out ghostly white; the fingers of her right hand played with the scar on her face, dancing jerkily over the trail left by her assailant's knife, from top to bottom, over and over.

Becca's heart went out to the thin, almost skeletal, woman sitting across from her, her pale blue eyes downcast, her gaze fixed on floor. Involuntary tremors shook her body, and she took in air in short, fast pants.

"I don't think I can do this," she whispered. She glanced briefly at Becca and then back down, shaking her head slowly from side to side. "I'm sorry." Her breathing sped up, grew yet more erratic. She appeared to be on the verge of passing out.

"Take a deep breath," Becca told her. "Nice and slow. In, one, two, three, four. Hold it. Out, one, two, three, four. That's it. Again. That's good. You're doing fine. In…and out…and now let your stomach go soft. Good. In…and out…and loose…and let your shoulders sag. That's right. And out…and let your jaw drop. Very good." She matched her own breathing to Ann's. "And what's a color that is safe and peaceful to you?"

"Pale yellow."

"And now, when you breathe in, imagine that you are breathing in pale yellow light. Let it fill you up, from the top of your head to the tip of your toes. In…and out, calm and peaceful, lighter and looser with every breath. That's right." Becca noted that the other woman's breathing had deepened and settled into a slow, rhythmic pattern. Her eyelids had drifted down, fluttered, and closed.

"And now let that pale yellow light push outward from every pore of your body, so that it extends into the space around you about a foot, in every direction, until you are surrounded by a shield of soft, yellow light." Becca saw the same yellow light filling and surrounding her, connecting her to Ann. She felt a twinge of guilt, knowing that she was going to disappoint Jack this time. What Jack wanted and what Ann Wilson needed were in conflict. He wanted more memories, detailed memories that would help him catch the rapist. Ann didn't need to retrieve memories; she needed to contain them until she'd learned how to manage her intense, overwhelming feelings. The woman was at serious risk for decompensating. Becca would bet her bank account that Ann had been the victim of childhood sexual abuse and repressed it. The recent trauma had ripped the lid off the box into which she'd stuffed the earlier one, and now she was well beyond her ability to cope.

Well, she'd made it clear in the beginning that her first loyalty was to the rape victims, not to the police department. Jack would understand, or he wouldn't.

"Rest in the light as long as you want. You have all the time you need. There is nowhere else you need to be and nothing else you need to do right now. You can let yourself relax and feel safe."

After a few minutes, Becca anchored the feeling for Ann so she could summon it at will by placing the tip of her pointer finger to the end of her thumb and thinking the word "yellow." She suggested Ann practice the visualization several times throughout the day and again at night when she wanted to go to sleep.

Following the anchoring exercise, Becca told Ann that they'd done enough for one day. Ann's eyes were clearer and less haunted, and she seemed much calmer than she had when she'd arrived. Her hand rested lightly on her husband's arm, and she stood straighter, without leaning into him. At the door, Jim Wilson smiled warmly at Becca and said, "Thank you for helping Annie."

She was spared having to defend her decision to Jack when his cell phone rang. He took the call, and five seconds into it, he was sprinting for his Jeep.

****

Jack slapped the emergency flasher on the roof of the Jeep and hit the gas. With any luck, he'd beat the ambulance to St. Theresa Hospital. According to

Courtney, their mother had taken a bad fall and was en route to the emergency room right now. Their father was out of town on business—what else was new?—and someone needed to handle the admission paper work and talk to the doctors. Courtney, seven months pregnant with her third, had her hands full with five-year-old Brandon and two-year-old Olivia.

"Has she been drinking?" he'd asked, knowing as he'd asked it that it was a dumb question. Was the Pope Catholic? Did summer follow spring? Had Kathleen Conroy been drinking?

"She's skunked," his sister had answered.

And didn't that sum up his happy family dynamics? Everything had fallen apart when Megan had been murdered. Christopher Conroy had lost himself in work, and Kathleen Conroy had lost herself in a bottle of Chardonnay. He and Courtney were nothing but painful reminders of the child who'd died. Some families drew closer together when tragedy struck. Others disintegrated. The Conroys had been one of the latter.

He pulled into the parking lot outside the emergency room and cut the engine. His mother wouldn't be glad to see him. She blamed him for Megan's death. He couldn't fault her for that; he blamed himself, too.

****

Becca was so pretty, and she had a smile that could light up a room; he knew because he'd seen it enough times. She wasn't smiling now, though. She was very somber as she gazed into the camera and urged women to take safety precautions to protect themselves. He hated seeing the worry lines around her mouth and knowing that he'd put them there. He wished he could reassure her, let her know that innocent women had nothing to fear from him.

The evil ones, on the other hand, should be quaking in their shoes because all the good advice in the world wouldn't be enough to spare them from their divine fate if the finger of God pointed at them.

In the beginning, he'd resisted his calling. Lord forgive him, but he hadn't wanted to serve. At the start, had he said, "Here am I, Lord, send me?" To his shame, he hadn't. He'd actually questioned his own sanity! He hadn't understood then, and he hadn't wanted to be the instrument through which God wrought His justice.

He wasn't resisting any longer. Tomorrow, God would show him who was next. Wednesday would be Judgment Day, and another pretender would be exposed and punished, another evil woman would face her Maker. He'd make sure of it.

Chapter Six

Sunday, February 12th

Becca stood outside the entrance of Church of the Lamb, where she was to meet Georgie and her husband, Harold. It seemed that she'd been waiting forever, but unless her watch had quit working, it had only been a few minutes. Organ music wafted through the doors every time a new arrival went into the sanctuary, and she gritted her teeth against the sound.

Almost everyone who passed her smiled and spoke. She smiled back, feeling like a hypocrite, and wishing she were anywhere else. If she hadn't promised Georgie she'd be there to lend her moral support, she'd get in her car and drive back home. She and God weren't on speaking terms and hadn't been since Kevin had succumbed to the voices the first time. What was the point in praying when God was, as far as she could tell, stone cold deaf? None of her prayers had ever been answered, that was for sure. As far as she was concerned, God had made it clear that she was on her own.

But this wasn't about her and God, she reminded herself. This was about her and Georgie, whose cap of bright red curls she could now see coming toward her from the parking lot.

"Thanks so much for being here," Georgie said as

she drew near. "This way, if I have a nervous breakdown, you can do some crisis intervention and prop me back up." She gave Becca a hug and then turned to the man beside her. "Honey, this is Becca Bennett, who's holding the fort down at Call Rape while Eileen is on maternity leave. Becca, this is my husband, Harold."

"Pleased to meet you." Becca shook hands with Georgie's tall, heavyset husband.

"You're in safe hands now. I've promised Georgie I'll not let anyone bite you this morning." He winked. "Now, if you come back a second time, I can't guarantee a thing, though far as I know we don't have any vampires on our membership rolls."

Becca laughed and followed Georgie inside. The sanctuary, shaped in a semicircle, was the largest she'd ever seen, and enough people had gathered to constitute a small city. A half dozen projection screens hung from the ceiling so the pulpit and the choir behind it could be clearly seen from every seat. Her church, from which she'd been absent the last dozen years, had a small, cozy sanctuary with dark wood pews on either side of a center aisle and brightly colored stained glass windows depicting a variety of Biblical scenes. There were no stained glass windows in Church of the Lamb. Instead, clear glass panels stretched from floor to ceiling letting the sunlight stream in from three sides, and showcasing huge hanging ferns. There were no pews, either. Individual, auditorium-style padded chairs filled six seating sections.

Becca tried to slide into a seat in the back next to David, a Friday afternoon volunteer at the Day Center for the Homeless, who gave her a big smile, but

Georgie caught her arm and steered her to the front of the center section. On their way down the aisle, she saw a few more people she knew. Betty Thomson, her mother's elderly neighbor, sat next to her oldest son. Jessica Alvarez, a former client, nodded at her. Tom and Millie Petrie from the soup kitchen waved at her. Seeing the two of them reminded her of Jeremy and with the thought of Jeremy came the realization that she'd missed Todd's art show yesterday. She almost smacked herself in the forehead. She'd call Todd this afternoon and apologize.

The first four rows were already full Georgie took the aisle seat in the fifth row. Harold took his place next to her. Becca sat on Harold's left. Almost immediately they all stood for two women who looked enough alike to be mother and daughter as they entered the row and sat next to Becca. Minutes later, the choir members rose. The song they sang was so lively and upbeat that Becca couldn't help herself; she tapped her toes. She decided that if there were a heaven, these people should be placed in charge of the music.

The Reverend William Bonner wasn't at all what she'd expected. He was unusually soft-spoken and mild mannered, as opposed to the forceful, energetic style she'd anticipated. He was also extraordinarily handsome, with just a touch of gray at his temples and the most vivid blue eyes she'd ever seen. His sermon, on the challenges of holding fast to faith in the face of unanswered prayer, hit close enough to home that it seemed he'd been listening in on her private thoughts.

After the offering had been taken and the anthem sung, Georgie made her way to the podium. When she turned to face the congregation, her gaze rested first on her husband and then on Becca. Becca gave her a discreet thumbs-up.

"When I was sixteen years old and a sophomore in high school, the most popular boy in the senior class asked me out," Georgie began. "I'd had a crush on him since the eighth grade, and I was deliriously happy. The invitation was to the movies, to be followed by a milkshake at Pennington's Drive-In, which was the "in" place at the time.

"Instead of the movies, though, he took me to a party. I was the youngest one there. Most of the others were juniors or seniors, a few had already graduated from high school. I was flattered that he thought I was mature enough, sophisticated enough, to be included. When the alcohol came out, I accepted the drink he handed me, and when he urged me to have a second, I took that one, too. I wanted him to like me." Her voice broke. "It was my first real date, and I'd swooned over him for three years, and I really, really wanted him to like me. I wanted him to kiss me, too, and when he did, I was thrilled." Her eyes glistened with tears.

"A lot about that night is a big blank. We were kissing in the living room, and the next thing I remember we were in a back bedroom, and he was on top of me. I tried to shove him off, but I couldn't. I said, 'No. Stop.' And he laughed. I started to cry. He got mad and backhanded me so hard that my front tooth punctured my lower lip." She touched her fingers to her mouth.

"He said, 'You've been begging for it all night. You know you want it. Don't you?' I didn't answer, and he hit me again. He kept hitting me and saying 'Don't you?' until I said 'Yes.'

"I didn't tell anyone what had happened to me. I was too ashamed. I thought it was my fault because I went to the party with him, because I got drunk, because I kissed him. It was almost twenty years before I heard the term 'date rape.' I never went back to school. I couldn't face him or any of the other people who were at that party. I'd been a four-point student with dreams of going to medical school, and then I was a high school dropout. I'd wanted to save lives, and then I wanted to die.

"If my story were an isolated one, I wouldn't be standing up here telling y'all about it. But the statistics are, in the course of her lifetime, one woman in three is a victim of rape, and a goodly number of those victims are teenage girls. Many of them are sexually assaulted by someone they know, like I was, a boyfriend, or a friend, or a classmate. One in twenty will commit suicide, or try to. More than that will turn to alcohol or drugs to escape the pain.

"We have a wonderful support group at the rape crisis center, but the young ones don't often come to that group. They need a group of their own. It's our dream at Call Rape to hire a part-time counselor who will work with teen rape victims and who will provide both girls and boys with education about sexual assault and its aftermath.

"I ask you to open your hearts to these young girls. I ask you to bless them twice, once with your prayers and again with your financial gifts. I know from my own personal experience that each one of them has been plunged straight into hell. The church represents the body of Christ in the world: let us reach out our hand to the young ones who have been damaged by sexual violence. If you're with me, say Amen."

"Amen," the congregation roared.

All around her Becca heard people shifting in their pews as they pulled wallets out of back pockets and retrieved checkbooks from purses. She got out her own checkbook.

"You were wonderful," Becca whispered when Georgie returned to her seat, leaning around Harold to hug her.

After the conclusion of the service, hordes of people surrounded Georgie, telling her how much her words had touched them and thanking her for sharing her story. Several women said they'd had similar experiences. Others asked about volunteer opportunities at Call Rape.

They were slowly edging their way toward the door when Becca caught sight of a familiar profile at the back of the sanctuary. Kevin! Her heart raced as adrenaline jolted her system in waves. Was that Kevin? She fought her way through the crowd to the place where the man had been standing, but by the time she got there, he was gone.

She ran out the big double doors and scanned the people outside, some standing around in small groups talking, most streaming toward the parking lot. No Kevin. If it had even been Kevin she'd seen. She couldn't be sure. She'd had just the one brief glimpse.

Weak with disappointment, she walked slowly to her car.

****

He'd freaked out when Becca had gone down to the front and taken her seat in row five. *Please, Lord, not Becca*, he'd prayed. When the other two women had stopped at the aisle, his heart had been in his throat. He'd been so afraid that Becca and her companions would move down two seats that he'd almost thrown up right there in God's house. He couldn't draw in any air at all, hadn't breathed again until those two women had taken seats four and five.

It had been a test of his faith and his commitment, he realized now. Because for those few minutes, he'd been filled with doubt. For those few minutes, he'd thought he'd been wrong about God's will for him. No, admit it, for those few minutes he'd been in rebellion, willing to defy the Lord Himself. It had been a test, like Abraham's willingness to sacrifice Isaac, and he'd failed that test. *Forgive me, Father.*

Shame bowed his head. No more doubt, he promised himself. No more rebellion. *Thy will, not mine*, he prayed, and instantly felt a river of peace running through his veins. Whatever God asked of him, he would do; even kill Becca, if that was the sacrifice the Lord demanded.

If Becca was good, which he sincerely believed she was, she would not be the target of God's wrath. What could be the harm in reassuring her that she had nothing to fear? There were so few good women—truly, hadn't the woman Eve started all the trouble in the first place by inviting evil into the world of humans?—those few who were the exception to the rule shouldn't be afraid.

He'd write her a letter, he decided, and explain his mission to her. She would understand; she was a very understanding person.

****

Monday, February 13th

She'd overslept, a rare thing for her, and now she

was running late, an even rarer occurrence. Becca hated the feeling, the little rush of adrenaline that came with hurrying and the scattered thoughts that jumped ahead, bounced back, ricocheted off each other.

She forced herself to slow down. Her first appointment wasn't until nine; she wasn't keeping anyone waiting. She just preferred to get to the office before eight, have a leisurely cup of coffee, review her schedule for the day, and get all her little ducks in a row. She liked her days orderly and predictable, doubtless a hangover from the chaos of her early childhood when any damn thing could happen at any time, and often did.

She'd overslept this morning because she'd dreamed about Kevin all night. She'd catch sight of him at the mall, but by the time she got to where he'd been standing, he'd be gone. She'd be certain she saw him walking ahead of her on Cherry Street and run to catch up, but her feet were heavy and her legs slow, and he'd turn a corner and disappear. She'd catch a glimpse of him out of the edge of her eye, blink, and he was no longer there. In her dreams she was in a school, in a grocery store, in a car, and she'd see a man she thought was Kevin, but she couldn't be sure, and try as she might, she was never fast enough or alert enough to reach him.

She knew what all that dreaming was about. Even in her sleep, she was haunted by her inability to find her brother. She wondered again if it had been Kevin she'd seen yesterday morning at the back of the sanctuary. She'd recreated those brief moments of hope and helpless despair over and over all night long.

Enough. She was exhausted and running behind

schedule, and she hadn't even left her house yet. Not a good way to start out her day. She brushed some blush across her cheeks and dabbed on some lipstick, slipped into a pair of charcoal gray slacks, and pulled on a black sweater, shoved her stocking feet into a pair of black loafers and retrieved her car keys, grabbed her coat and her briefcase, and flew out the door. She'd make it to work by eight thirty, maybe even eight twenty-five.

She came to an abrupt stop a few feet from her car. A folded sheet of white paper was trapped between the windshield and the wiper on the driver's side. Heart thumping erratically, she tugged it free and read the typed letter that began "Dearest Becca."

And then, heart pounding so hard it felt in danger of exploding right out of her chest and fingers shaking so badly that she dropped her purse twice before she managed to get to her cell phone, she called Jack Conroy.

****

"Dearest Becca,

Appearances can be deceiving. Sometimes evil appears as it is, but more often it is disguised by the mask of goodness. A pretty face, a soft voice, a graceful carriage, these are common masks. Humans are fooled by the mask, but God sees the heart. Women are predisposed to immorality. Read your Bible to know I speak the truth. It was Eve who ate that apple and urged Adam to do the same. Adam was weak, as men tend to be, but Eve was wicked, as women tend to be. Are all women wicked? No. You, I believe, are an exception to the rule, and that's why I'm writing—to put your mind at rest. Do not grieve for the women who have been punished. Beneath their masks, they were the ugliest of evil. I do not know who will be next as it is God, not I, who chooses. But to you, Dearest Becca, I say, Fear not. To all others, I say, Repent, before it is too late."

Jack read the letter twice and then slipped it into a clear plastic evidence bag and stripped off thin latex gloves. He used his cell phone to make arrangements for a crime scene technician to dust the letter and the windshield wiper of the Civic for fingerprints as soon as he and Becca got to the station. Then he called Sully, who promised to be there inside of fifteen minutes and to bring two uniforms with him to help with the door-to-doors.

Becca had been white as chalk when he'd arrived and shaking like a leaf in a storm. Of course, she'd insisted that she was fine, so he'd gone along with her and pretended that she was fine, when what he'd wanted to do was gather her in his arms and soothe her. He'd wanted to tuck her head into his shoulder and smooth his hand down her back, at least until she quit trembling, but he hadn't because he knew all about faking fine. He knew it was warmth and kindness that shattered defenses, knew she wouldn't appreciate it at all if her façade cracked. So he gave her what she needed to maintain it, which was distance and a matter-of-fact response.

Instead of comforting her, he'd snapped on a pair of latex gloves, picked up the letter from the hood of the car where it had fallen when she'd dropped it, and read the message the killer had sent Becca. Then he'd told her she needed to come down to the station to get printed so they could eliminate her prints on the paper, and she'd have to hang around a little bit and answer some questions. Lips compressed, she'd nodded her agreement. It had been as clear to her as it was to him that the killer was someone she knew. She'd rescheduled her first two appointments of the day without protest.

"I'll be right behind you," he said, opening her car door and waiting for her to get in.

She slid into the driver's seat and then just sat there. The lines around her mouth drew tighter and the furrow in the middle of her forehead deepened. The vacant look in her eyes had him second guessing himself. Maybe she didn't need to be behind the wheel of a car.

"Give me the keys and scoot over," he said. "I'll drive."

That snapped her out of it, not that snapping her out of it had been his intention. She straightened and refocused her gaze on him.

"I'll drive," she said, inserting the key into the ignition and twisting, lifting her foot to the brake pedal, and putting the car into reverse.

"Wait." He leaned down and grabbed the seatbelt, pulled it across her, and fastened it with a click. Big mistake. That close, he could smell her unique scent, and it made him want to stay right where he was and just breathe her in until she filled him up inside. If he turned his head to the right and lowered it a mere two inches, he could trace her soft lips with his tongue, learn the taste and texture of her mouth.

God in heaven, what was he thinking? He was in the middle of a murder investigation, not to mention the fact that the woman had made it perfectly clear that kissing him was not on her agenda. He jerked backward so quickly that he almost lost his balance and had to steady himself with a hand on the steering wheel.

Great. He not only went stupid around her, now he was turning into a klutz, too. She didn't seem to notice, though, and he was grateful for that small favor from the universe. He took a step back, straightened, and shut her car door.

Becca had the car in drive instead of reverse and almost rear-ended Jack's Jeep before she got it stopped and back into park.

"I'll drive," Jack said. "We'll take my car. I'll send one of the tech guys for yours." This time she didn't protest, she just scrambled out of the Honda and into the passenger seat of his Jeep without a word, hated feeling relieved that he was taking charge and feeling it just the same.

He buckled her in again after she fumbled the seatbelt the second time, and once he got them out on the road, he threaded his fingers between hers, rested their clasped hands on his right thigh, and said, "It'll be okay."

She clung to his hand and his words, grateful for both. His reassuring presence beside her held her steady and kept her from losing the tenuous grip she had on her composure. His strength reminded her that she needed to be strong, too.

Because, no question about it, the man who'd written to her was the same man who'd been raping and killing women the last five weeks. She felt cold all the way to the bone at the knowledge that the killer had picked her to explain himself to and in her mind the finger of guilt was pointing right at Kevin. She didn't want to believe it, in her heart she couldn't believe it, but who else except Kevin would feel the need to enlighten and reassure her? And the religiosity of the letter sounded like Kevin's voices when he'd gone too long without his meds.

Of course, she thought with a mirthless chuckle, Tulsa probably had the highest concentration of religious nuts in the known universe. Kevin was hardly the only one in town who heard the voice of God whispering in his ear. A person could barely turn around without bumping into someone who thought he or she had a private line straight to the top and wanted to tell everyone within hearing distance where they were stepping off the one, true path. If she had a dime for every time someone had tried to "save" her, persuade her, or witness to her, she could retire right now, buy an island in the South Pacific, and live out her life in luxury. And while she wasn't afraid of her brother, if Kevin was innocent—well, of course he was innocent. The note from him had been handwritten on a grocery sack, and this one had been typed. Her heart soared at that thought, but then she remembered that there were computers available to the public at both the library and the Day Center, and it plummeted again. She wanted Kevin to be innocent, and if he was, that meant someone else had written her that letter. Taking comfort from the man beside her she held tighter to his hand. There was no one she'd rather have standing between her and a deranged killer than Jack Conroy.

He parked three rows over and eight cars down from the entrance to the police station and they just sat there for a minute. She took in a deep breath, slowly, and let it out slowly.

Her fear of being fingerprinted was irrational, and she knew it. She wasn't in the system and fingerprints wouldn't reveal the secret of her identity. She closed her eyes and drew in another slow breath, reaching for an inner calm that was nowhere to be found, and when she opened them, Jack rubbed her hand between his and then released her to unfasten the seatbelt. She wrapped her shaking fingers around the door handle, shoved, and stepped out of the relative safety of his Jeep.

He took her arm, just above the elbow, guiding her through the parking lot, and his touch calmed her. How could that be? It didn't make sense that the one man who should have sent her already jittery nerves into anxious spasms was the one to still them. She was cold through and through, and she wanted to warm her body against his heat. She resisted the urge to lean into him, lean on him. She'd never leaned on anyone in her life, and she wasn't starting now. She must really be losing it. It was too weird that Jack Conroy, of all people, could quiet her fear, something no one else had ever managed to do, but weird beat scared spitless by a country mile. She let him lead her inside the building, down a hallway, through a large room, and into a smaller one with just enough room for a rectangular table in the middle surrounded by a few beige metal folding chairs. He pulled out a chair for her and she sat.

"Coffee?"

"No, thanks." She thought if she put anything in her stomach now, it might come right back up.

"Be right back." He disappeared, and she looked at unadorned beige walls, broken only by the door through which they'd entered and a mirror. Must be an interview room, she thought. It was creepy to think someone could be on the other side watching her this very minute, and she'd never know it.

Jack reappeared with a mug full of coffee, from which he took a sip, and sat opposite her. He pulled a small spiral notebook and pencil out of his shirt pocket.

She went over the basics again: She'd left her house at 8:17, she'd found the note on her windshield maybe thirty seconds later, she'd read it through once, called him, and waited for him to arrive.

"It's someone you know," he stated, "or at least it's someone who knows you. Let's put our heads together and see if we can figure out who it is."

Her mouth was so dry she couldn't speak, so she simply nodded. She should have taken him up on that offer of coffee. She glanced at the mug. Maybe she'd just help herself to some of his.

As if he'd read her mind he pushed it a few inches in her direction. "I'll share, if you change your mind."

She picked it up and took a swallow. Better. She took another swallow and returned the mug to the center of the table. "Thanks."

He led her through a typical week, day by day, and before she knew it he'd written down the names of most of her friends in his little notebook. Tom, Joe, and Jeremy from the soup kitchen, and Jeremy's partner, Todd, all made it onto the list. So did David from the Day Center for the Homeless, and Brandon, her neighbor three doors down. Kevin's name was conspicuously absent, but she knew he'd made Jack's mental inventory because he'd asked more questions about him and his mental health problems and the voices he heard. She couldn't take offense because, even though it made her feel like a traitor, Kevin's name was on her list, too.

"What about clients?" he asked, pencil poised.

"Most of my clients are women," she said.

"But not all."

She thought about Doug, grieving the death of his only child, a son, and Peter, struggling with severe anxiety and panic attacks. She couldn't picture either of them in the role of rapist/murderer. Or Chad, who struggled with crippling depression. Or any of the others.

"No, not all. Even if I thought one of my male clients might be a possible suspect, which I most certainly do not, I couldn't violate patient confidentiality by giving you their names, not when the only reason to do so is because they are my clients."

She thought Jack was going to argue with her, could see the internal debate in the annoyed tapping of his pencil and the narrowing of his eyes, but after he heaved out an irritated sigh he dropped it.

"How about boyfriends, ex-boyfriends, and wannabe boyfriends?"

There hadn't been that many, in any of the above categories, but she gave him all their names, feeling more disloyal and more vulnerable with every breath. The very process of looking at everyone she knew as a possible killer made her feel as weak and helpless as she'd felt as a little girl, and she hated it. She hated looking at the world through suspicious eyes, hated questioning the motives of every man with whom she'd come into contact, hated being scared. She'd worked hard to overcome all that and now she was right back there, where she'd sworn never to be again. Abruptly she shoved away from the table and to her feet.

"I'll let you know if I think of anyone else." She grabbed her purse and started for the door. "Right now I have clients to see, people who are counting on me." And that was a fact she'd do well to remember. Just saying it made her feel better, more like herself.

"Wait." Jack stopped her with a hand on her forearm. "We're not finished. Sit back down."

She just looked at him.

"He'll contact you again, and we need to be prepared."

His words penetrated, and all the air whooshed out of her lungs. She sat down hard. Of course he'd contact her again. Why hadn't she thought of that? She gripped her purse tightly in an effort to still her shaking hands. Fear twisted her stomach into a hard knot, made her lightheaded and dizzy.

"Becca?" Jack slid his hand down to her wrist and then turned it so that their palms pressed together. "You with me?"

She looked into his blue eyes and took a deep breath, nodded.

"Good." He squeezed her hand. "I'd like to put a tap on your home phone. You okay with that?"

She felt so cold and the only warm place on her entire body was where his hand touched hers. His steady gaze was a visual lifeline, and she clung to it.

"Yes."

"I'll take care of that then. And I'll arrange for some drive-bys during the evenings and nights. If he calls you, keep him on the phone as long as you can. If you get another letter, let me know right away. If anything, or anyone, seems off, call me and I'll be there, anytime, night or day. Okay?"

"Okay. Thanks." She straightened her shoulders. She would not feel like a victim again. "Anything I can do to help you catch him, I'll do."

"I'll check with Fred and see if he's finished with your car."

He used his cell phone and even though she could only hear his side of the short conversation she knew the answer before he told her.

"After we get you fingerprinted, I'll drop you off at your office. Fred promises you'll have your car back sometime this afternoon. I'll get it to you as soon as I can."

Their hands were still entwined, and even though she knew she should withdraw hers, the skin to skin contact with him felt so good, so reassuring, that she didn't do it.

A young woman with flyaway red hair and a multitude of freckles came through the door. "Hey, Detective," she said, smiling at Jack.

"Hey, Kristen," Jack responded. "This is Rebecca Bennett. Becca, Kristen Lauer. She's here to get your fingerprints."

"No need to get up," Kristen said when Becca started to rise. She laid two white cards on the table, placed two small squares of black paper next to them, unhooked an ink pen from the neck of her blouse, and turned her smile on Becca. "Let me just get the basics first: name, address, date of birth, social security number. Then we'll ink you up."

Becca hadn't thought she could get colder, but Kristen's words were like a bucket of ice down the back of her sweater. Her imagination took her back to that night over twenty years ago when her father had rushed out of their house the last time and shortly thereafter raped and killed Megan Conroy. The police had arrested him and brought him to this very place. Doubtless they'd fingerprinted him before they'd locked him in a cell. *Stay away from cops. They mess with people just for kicks. Makes them feel important. Never tell them anything, even your name.* Preparing to have her fingerprints taken, she'd never felt more her father's daughter. She could hear his voice, traveling through the years, issuing the admonishment he'd given her almost daily, and she felt an unreasoning impulse to flee. *Stop*, she silently ordered.

Fear clogged her throat, but she managed to push the words out, giving Kristen the information, which she wrote down on first one card and then the other. She clipped the pen back onto her blouse and reached for Becca's right hand. She carefully rolled each finger over the black paper and pressed it to a square on one of the cards.

"One down, one to go," she said cheerfully and then repeated the process with Becca's left hand. She slid the two cards into an envelope, pulled a package of wipes out of her pocket and handed several of them to Becca. "This'll get you cleaned up." With another smile and a perky little wave of her hand, she departed.

Becca tried to use the wipes, but her fingers were frozen, so cold they were numb, and she dropped them. Jack bent down to pick them up.

"Let me do that for you." He captured one hand in his and ran the wipe over the tips of her fingers, then did the same with her other hand and dropped the wipes on the table.

"You're freezing." He clasped both of her hands between his and rubbed briskly. The friction created a soothing heat, and his intense gaze warmed more than her hands.

She was so unaccustomed to being fussed over that she felt disoriented. She stood there, looking up into his blue eyes while he rubbed her hands, and she was helpless to move away even though that was what she kept telling herself she should do. It was a little thing, really, rubbing her hands, but she felt taken care of, and it was so foreign to her, being taken care of, that she was rooted to the spot. She was always the caregiver, not the care receiver, and she'd had no idea before right this minute how much she'd craved just this.

She might have stood there forever, but his cell phone rang. Without lifting his gaze from hers, he pulled it out of his pocket and flipped it open.

"Conroy." A slow smile spread over his face. "Thanks, Zach. We'll meet you there in five." He slid the phone back into his pocket, still smiling, and turned her to the door. He draped an arm across her shoulders.

"What?" she asked. "Where are we going?"

"Utica Psychiatric Center." His smile broadened. "Officer Brewer is heading that way right now. With your brother."

Chapter Seven

Monday, February 13th

While Becca had been freezing just moments ago, she was now zinging back and forth between hot and cold with the speed of a tennis ball at Wimbledon. She thought of Kevin, safe at last, and relief flooded her with heat. She thought of the killer still at large and fear scraped an icy finger down her spine. She thought of Kevin, found guilty of heinous crimes and her family back in the public spotlight and burned with shame. She thought of another letter or a phone call from an unknown killer and went numb with cold. She thought of the joy her mother and Cara would feel—she'd call as soon as she saw him with her own eyes and knew positively it was Kevin—and love warmed her from the inside. She thought about Jack discovering her brother's—and her—true identity and felt hot and cold at the same time.

Jack still had his arm around her shoulders, and the reassuring weight of it kept her grounded even as they hustled to his Jeep. The right side of her body pressed against his, and the sheer solidity of him comforted her.

"Is he sure it's Kevin?" she asked again.

"Pretty sure. We'll know, one way or the other, in about ten minutes."

He unlocked the Jeep, and she slid into the

passenger seat. She didn't know if she could stand the suspense for another ten minutes. Hope that her six-week long nightmare was about to come to an end warred with the fear that the nightmare might be just beginning.

Jack maneuvered the vehicle out of the parking garage, and her right foot pressed the floorboard as if she might speed up their progress, but as soon as they were out on the street her left foot pressed hard, as if she might be able to slow them down. It was a good thing she wasn't the one behind the wheel she thought, or they'd be alternately shooting forward and slamming to a stop all the way across town.

"Almost there," Jack said. "Breathe, before you pass out."

She was holding her breath, she realized, and drew in a deep lungful of air.

"If it's not him this time, we'll keep looking." He stroked the back side of her hand, and she became conscious that it was fisted in her lap.

By an act of will, she relaxed her fingers and stilled her foot, which she noticed was again pushing against the floorboard. Could this car not go any faster? Good Lord, she might get there quicker if she jumped out and ran the rest of the way.

But when they pulled up outside the hospital and parked, she was unable to move at all. Her legs were heavy weights, holding her in place. Her fingers, clenched once more, were too stiff to work the door handle. She'd gone beyond cold to frozen. It took Jack, opening her door and clasping her hands to help her out of the car, to get her moving again. Once her feet hit the pavement, though, a burst of adrenaline pushed her whole system into overdrive. She streaked across the parking lot like a race car bearing down on the finish line, feeling like her heart was going three thousand rpm.

She forgot all about Jack until she arrived at the entrance and his hand reached around her to shove open the door. She burst into the waiting room and slowed to a crawl when she saw that it was empty. Jack strode past her to the receptionist's window and hit a buzzer on the wall beside it. A young woman, model thin and carefully made up, appeared on the other side of the window and slid the glass open.

"May I help you, sir?"

"Detective Conroy, here to meet Officer Brewer."

"Through those doors"—she gestured with a wave of her hand—"third office on your right. I'll buzz you in."

The doors opened with a click and a pneumatic hiss. The receptionist turned her attention to Becca.

"May I help you, ma'am?"

"She's with me." Jack caught Becca's elbow and pushed through the double doors, taking her with him.

She heard Kevin before she saw him. He was shouting scripture, something about the Lord delivering him from his enemies, and demanding to be released. His voice sounded angry, but she knew him well enough to know that underneath the anger was overwhelming fear. She broke into a run.

She rounded the doorframe into the room. A man with wire rim glasses, doubtless a psychiatrist, sat behind a desk. A uniformed officer, tall and lean and looking like he'd be more comfortable in a pair of Levis and cowboy boots, stood between the desk and the door. She scanned the rest of the room and spied Kevin. He was skeletal thin, and her eyes teared at the sight. He stood in the corner, back pressing against the wall, arms crossed over his narrow torso. His chest heaved and red splotches covered his face. He was on the verge of a panic attack. His eyes widened as she approached him, murmuring soothing reassurances.

"Stay away," he yelled. "Danger. Danger."

She wrapped her arms around him, and he recoiled from her touch, jerking away and sliding down the wall to land in a heap on the floor at her feet.

"It's okay, Kevin." She bent down and rested a hand on his shoulder. He squeezed his eyes tightly shut.

"The doctor and the rest of the staff here will help you, Kevin. You'll be okay."

"Red alert," he whispered.

Red alert had been their childhood code for "Watch out for Dad." At one time they'd both believed that their father was sometimes taken over by aliens. How else to explain the abrupt changes, the lightning quick shifts in mood, the rapid swing from fun and loving to mean and scary?

"He can't hurt you any more, Kevin," she said. "He's gone. Remember? You're safe now."

"Not him. *Me*." His eyes popped open, and his anguished gaze took her breath away. "So *you're* not safe now. Go away."

She tried again to comfort him, but he twisted away from her. He covered his ears with his hands, banged his head on the floor and started screaming, "Get her away from me. Somebody get her away from me."

The psychiatrist rose and motioned with his head

for her to step outside the room. He followed her into the hall.

"If you can stay until we get him settled in, I'd like to talk with you."

"I'll stay. I'd like to talk with you, too. I'll be in the reception area."

She cast one last glance at Kevin, quiet now, but still with his eyes closed and his hands clapped over his ears. She left the room at a much slower pace than she'd entered it. In all the times he'd disappeared in the past, Kevin had always been glad to see her when they found him. She didn't understand why he wanted nothing to do with her now. *He's psychotic. Quit trying to make sense out of it. Just be glad he's still alive and safe.* Which, she thought with a deep wave of thankfulness, he wouldn't be if it weren't for Jack Conroy. To whom she hadn't yet expressed any appreciation for finding her brother.

She'd just passed through the doors into the waiting room when that realization struck her. She turned around abruptly and ran smack into the hard wall of his chest. The rush of gratitude had her wrapping her arms around his waist.

"Thank you." She punctuated her words with a squeeze. "I've been so worried about him, so scared for him, we all have, and it's such a wonderful relief to know he's okay, and I can't say it enough, thank you."

"You're welcome. Glad I could help." His breath tickled her forehead when he spoke. His arms came around her. He held her firmly against him, one hand pressing her head against his shoulder, the other slowly stroking her back from neck to waist. His voice was low, his body was warm, and his hands were gentle. His heart beat steady beneath her ear. Not until she relaxed and the trembling abated did she realize that she'd been shaking.

She sighed and breathed deeply, inhaling the fresh masculine scent of him. Her cheek nestled in the hollow below his collarbone as if that spot had been carved out just for her. Her awareness followed the slow smoothing of his palm down her back, expanded to encompass the firm muscles of his thighs pressing against hers and the delicious sensation of her breasts against his unyielding chest. Her skin seemed several sizes too small, and her muscles felt tense and achy. Her stomach tightened, and her nipples grew hard. Good grief, he was comforting her, and she was getting turned on. Embarrassed, she pulled away and took a big step back.

"It'll take a little while for the psychiatrist to evaluate Kevin and get him admitted to the unit, but you don't have to wait." She forced herself to meet his gaze. "My mom will be here as soon as I call her."

He studied her for a long minute, his blue eyes dark and searching, and then he nodded. "I'll let you know as soon as your car is ready."

****

Well, that had been nice while it had lasted. Rebecca Bennett was like a quarter horse—she could turn on a dime. One minute she was in his arms—where, every cell in his body had noted, she fit perfectly—and the next she was halfway across the room. She accepted consolation and then coolly dismissed him. She got his hopes, among other things, up and then squelched any optimism he might have that she could possibly like him, even a little, or be the tiniest bit attracted to him.

He was a moron to even be thinking about her and her many mood fluctuations. He didn't have time for this. He needed to be checking out all the names on the list they'd made, asking questions, knocking on doors, looking for witnesses, doing his job. Catching a killer. A killer who knew Becca. A killer who, Jack felt it in his gut, could switch from admiration to contempt in the blink of an eye. A killer who, for all Jack knew, could be this very second plotting how he was going to rape, torture, and kill Rebecca Bennett.

****

So when was she going to get her car back? The last appointment of the day had canceled and Becca was ready to go home. She felt like she'd been run over by a Mack truck. She'd been trying to get caught up on progress notes, but she couldn't concentrate she was so tired. Not so tired that her mind didn't keep going back to Kevin, though.

According to their mother, he'd been somewhat calmer when she'd seen him, but had gone berserk at the mere mention of Cara's name. He'd wanted Marie to promise she'd keep Cara away from him until the first day of the new year and warned her that she needed to be prepared to kill him if necessary, for Cara's sake. Over and over, he'd kept screaming, "Keep her away from me," and "Kill me. Promise you'll kill me."

Becca had been through this enough times to know that in just a few days, certainly by the weekend, Kevin would be rational again, at which time he might, or might not, be able to tell them why he'd left, where he'd been, and what he'd been thinking and doing during the last six weeks.

And even if those questions never got answered, the most important question of all would be laid to rest on Thursday whether Kevin spoke a single word or not. Because the rapist turned killer had struck every Wednesday night for the last five weeks. If a new victim was discovered on Thursday, Kevin would definitely be in the clear. On the other hand, if Thursday came and went with no new activity coming to light…

She shuddered and cut that thought off, refocusing on her current problem. She started loading files into her briefcase. She was giving Jack Conroy another ten minutes, and then she was calling. She'd no more had the thought than Denise buzzed her.

****

Jack had gotten so caught up in running down the names Becca had given him that he'd lost track of time. For reasons he didn't want to examine too closely, he'd started with the ex-boyfriends. He'd take another look at Stan Marshall tomorrow; there was something weasely about that guy. He'd marked both Bill Sampson and Steve Rollins off his list. The neighbor who'd asked her out several times, Brandon Grissom, had also checked out; he worked the 7:00 p.m.-7:00 a.m. shift at St. Theresa Hospital and had been working on three of the five Wednesdays in question.

"Earth to Conroy," Kristen Lauer said, handing him the key to Becca's car. "I'm off." She walked out the door with a smile and a little finger wave.

Time to get a move on. He shoved his notes into a file folder, which he tucked under his arm. He'd be going over all this at least one more time this evening, looking for anything that he might have missed, hoping something would jump out at him.

When he pulled up outside Becca's office, he was still wondering what was wrong with Bill Sampson, Steve Rollins, and Stan Marshall, that they'd let her get away. Not that their loss was going to be his gain. Unless one of the moods he hadn't seen yet was Jump Jack's Bones. Now that was a mood he'd love to see her in.

In your dreams, he told himself as he got out of the car. *Get over it.*

Inside, the receptionist gave him a conspiratorial wink. "You can go on back. Tell her I'm on my way out, and I'll see her in the morning."

He was going to have to talk to Becca about that. With the killer having singled her out for God only knew what reason, her receptionist was going to have to be a lot more vigilant.

He and Becca met up in the hallway just outside her private office. The emotional strain of the day had left tiny lines of tension around her mouth and leached the color out of her cheeks. It showed in the slowness of her steps and the droop of her shoulders. It was all he could do not to smooth those lines around her mouth with his thumb and tell her that everything was going to be okay. Like he knew whether anything was going to be okay or not.

"Here, let me carry that." He lifted the bulging briefcase out of her hand.

She didn't even protest, further evidence of her emotional exhaustion. She just let the weight of it shift from her hand to his and sighed.

"How's your brother doing?" he asked, just for

something to say. He knew the man wasn't going to be living in the real world in six hours time, no matter how many anti-psychotic meds the psychiatrist had pumped into his system.

"They had to wrestle him into restraints and give him a shot of Thorazine. I imagine he's sleeping right about now."

"You look like you could use a little sleep yourself." She looked like she was going to topple over any minute.

"Your receptionist said to tell you that she's on her way out, and she'll see you in the morning. Does she know about the letter you got today?"

Becca shook her head.

"You need to fill her in on everything. She needs to be a lot more cautious until this guy's caught. In fact, I'll get someone out here first thing tomorrow to get the ball rolling on installing an alarm with a buzzer at her desk and another one in your office, so all either of you has to do is hit it and the police will be on the way." The thought of the killer getting his hands on Becca put a knot the size of Texas in his stomach.

"I really don't think that's necessary." She began walking toward the waiting room.

"Have you never heard the adage 'Better safe than sorry'?"

"I'll think about it." Her tone was final.

"You do that." He would have pushed harder if he thought it would do any good, but her jaw was set, she'd straightened her back and squared her shoulders, and he quickly decided that a tactical retreat was in order. It went against the grain, and against his gut feeling that she could be in danger, but he kept his mouth shut. For now.

He followed her into the waiting room and saw that the receptionist was already gone. That woman sure was fast on her feet.

"When you talk to your helper in the morning, suggest that you and she arrive at the same time and leave at the same time."

Becca nodded, flicked off the last light, and pulled the door open. Counting that nod as a small victory, he stepped out onto the porch and waited while she locked up.

She looked out at the lot, empty save for his Jeep, and cast him a questioning glance.

"I couldn't find anyone who was free to follow and give me a ride back downtown." That was a lie. He'd wanted an excuse to spend a little more time with her. "So instead of delivering the car to you, I decided to deliver you to the car." He gave her his most winning smile, and eureka, she smiled back at him.

"So tell me about your brother," he said when they were settled in the car. "How old was he when he—" He stopped because he wasn't quite sure how to finish that question. *Turned into a fruit loop,* which had been his original thought, didn't seem like the best way to ask it.

"Had his first psychotic break?" she asked. "When he was nineteen. Halfway through the first semester of his sophomore year at OU, or at least that's when we found out about it. His roommate, Chad, called to tell us that Kevin hadn't left the room since the first four weeks into the semester. Chad had been bringing him food and collecting his mail. Then during the week of mid-terms, Kevin started hiding in the closet. He wouldn't eat the food Chad brought him any more and accused Chad of trying to poison him."

The expression of sadness on her face made something in his chest get tight. *Way to go, champ*, he congratulated himself. He hadn't meant to make her feel worse, but that's exactly what he'd done.

"Tell me about him before," he urged, and her features immediately brightened.

"Oh, growing up, Kevin was the best big brother ever. He always let me tag along, whatever he was doing. When Dad built a tree house for him, all his friends wanted it to be a boys-only club house, but Kevin insisted I be allowed to hang out in it, too. He taught me how to ride a bicycle, how to hit a baseball, and how to catch crawdads. If anyone was ever mean to me"—a shadow crossed her face—"he always stood up for me and he did his best to protect me."

"Sounds like the two of you were close."

"Very." She turned toward him and smiled, a genuine light-up-the-room smile, and the tightness in his chest disappeared. "He was my brother and my best friend and my hero. When the Seroquel kicks in, the difference will be amazing. He'll be back to his real self, sweet and funny and loving. Everyone will be so glad to have him home again."

"That'll be good." Impulsively he reached over and squeezed her hand. "I hope it's soon."

To his astonishment she turned her hand palm up and linked their fingers. After a few moments she said, "Thank you so much for finding my brother," and he said, "You're welcome," and still her hand nestled in his. It felt right. It felt like that's where her hand belonged—in his. If he'd known the rewards that finding her brother would yield, he'd have been out beating the bushes himself.

Her brother was a lucky man to have a sister who cared for him so deeply and so unconditionally. A fierce yearning welled up in him. What must it be like to be on the receiving end of that kind of love? He banished the thought the instant it was clearly formed. It was foolishness to want what you couldn't have and didn't deserve.

"So," he said, enjoying the feeling of her hand in his, "tell me about the rest of your family." After a brief pause, she started talking again.

"My mother is one of those people who make everything fun. Everything is a party. In the fall we had leaf raking parties. First we raked them all into big piles and then we ran and jumped into the piles. Then she served hot cider and cookies, and we all went back outside and bagged the leaves. She threw snow shoveling parties, weed pulling parties, house cleaning parties, you name it, and she turned it into a party.

"My dad is solid and steady. Nothing much upsets him. He's a very loyal, idealistic person who'd give you the shirt off his back if you needed it, and he'll stop what he's doing at the drop of a hat if you need to talk to him.

"And Cara, Kevin's daughter, is the light of all our lives. She's a lot like her dad and grandma in disposition, cheerful and pleasant and softhearted. When Kevin goes off his meds and disappears, it's really rough on her because she adores him. Luckily for her, they live with my folks, so when Kevin's messed up, my mom and dad take up the slack. She's ecstatic that he'll be home soon."

"Your family sounds nice." Hell, except for the schizophrenic brother, they sounded like the fricking Cleavers. He had a mental image of a Norman Rockwell family, gathered around the table for Thanksgiving dinner, everyone talking and laughing. It was a far cry from the Conroy family gatherings, such as they were. Maybe once a year Courtney managed to get them all together in one place for a meal. They counted it a success if their mother didn't get drunk and their father didn't leave early to get some work done.

"They are. None of us are perfect—except for Cara"—she grinned—"but I'm lucky to have them. Tell me about your folks."

"They're all right."

"All right?" She laughed. "Gee, you have a real way with words, Conroy. From that description, I feel like I practically know them."

"They're—" He cast about for some flattering things to say and then thought, *Screw it*. The truth was the truth. "They're both -ics. Dad's a workaholic, and Mom's an alcoholic." On the other hand, there was such a thing as too much information, and anything more would cross that line in his book. "My sister Courtney is delightful. She's very artistic; she draws and paints and plays the piano. She has her own unique viewpoint and an offbeat sense of humor. Her husband's a stand up guy, and they have a couple of pretty neat kids."

Thank God, they were back in the parking garage, and he could quit with the family documentary. He wasn't talking about Megan, not to Becca, not to anybody. Never had, never would.

"Here we are," he announced unnecessarily. He

pulled into the slot next to her Honda and cut the engine, relinquishing her hand at the very last minute. As soon as he let it go, he wanted it back again. He'd been enjoying touching her and getting to know her a little bit better, the feeling of closeness. He'd like to be friends with her. Okay, what he really like was for them to be friends who had wild monkey sex together. But who could predict—certainly not he—whether the next time they saw each other she'd be touchable or strictly hands off, warmly personal or coolly professional or even faintly adversarial.

With a sigh, he got out of the Jeep and retrieved her briefcase from the back seat. He fished her car key out of his pocket, popped the trunk on the Civic, and put the briefcase inside. He unlocked her car door and handed the key to her.

"Thanks again." She took the key and stood there, smiling up at him. Her liquid brown eyes were the color of melting dark chocolate, and he couldn't look away. His breath got hung up in his chest somewhere, and his heart beat like a bass drum. He thought, *What the hell. No guts, no glory*, and reached for her.

He framed her face with his hands and very slowly, very deliberately, lowered his head. He gave her plenty of time to move away, if she wanted to; his intentions were crystal clear. Instead, she let her head fall back and her eyes drift closed.

He brushed his lips across hers lightly, and then a second time and a third. So soft. He settled his mouth firmly over hers. He groaned as she kissed him back, and every muscle in his body hardened at the slight sucking sensations of her lips on his. He pressed down on her chin with his thumb and traced the seam of her lips with his tongue, and she opened to him. She tasted just the way he'd thought she would, sweet and spicy at the same time. He inhaled deeply, filling himself with the dark, mysterious woman scent of her.

Her taste and scent swam through his blood like a drug, taking him higher, making every cell in his body hum with pleasure. He probed her mouth with his tongue and smoothed one hand down the curve of her spine to press against the small of her back bringing her closer. Her arms, which had been resting against his chest, moved up around his neck, and her fingers burrowed through his hair.

The slow slide of her tongue against his produced the heat of a five-alarm fire. His heightened senses registered everything about her: the exotic taste; the musky scent; the warmth of her breath fanning his cheek; the soft, heavy curls of her hair beneath one palm and the curve of her hip against the other; the brush of her fingers on the back of his neck; the fullness of her breasts against his chest; the plump lower lip; the pressure of her thighs against his; the smooth shell of her ear under his thumb.

He pictured her naked, on satin sheets, the glow from a dozen candles highlighting the hills and valleys of her curves, her skin rosy and sweat slicked, her arms reaching for him, her legs opening as he covered her, the delicious friction of skin against bare skin, nothing between them except the heat their bodies generated.

The ear splitting honk of a car horn shattered the sensual haze that had him in its grip. He broke the kiss and turned his head to glower at the intruder, who turned out to be Sully, pulling to a stop beside them.

"Just got a call from a woman who spotted a

prowler outside her neighbor's bedroom window last night. She thinks the same man is sitting in a parked car down the block right now. Might be our guy. You wanna go?"

He turned back to Becca, still panting like he'd run the Boston Marathon, and rested his forehead on hers as he fought to bring his breathing under control. He didn't want to let her go. His arms felt empty already, and he hadn't turned her loose yet.

"I'll call you," he finally managed to get out.

"Not a word," he warned his friend as he slid into the passenger side of the Ford Taurus. "Not a single damn word."

****

Dazed, Becca sagged against the side of her car. Good Lord, that man could kiss. She wished she didn't know that. She really did. She touched her fingertips to her swollen lips and drew in a ragged breath.

She slid, practically boneless, into the car and then just sat there. How had that happened? Okay, she'd been wondering what it would be like to kiss him since the day he'd first appeared in her waiting room, but her imagination had fallen far short of the real thing. Still, she prided herself on her self control, and she'd never planned to act on her curiosity. Yet she'd known he was going to kiss her, and she hadn't been able to move away. And now she'd really stepped in it because that kiss was going to make it harder to do what she had to do.

Things had been going well, despite the emotional roller coaster she'd been riding all day. She'd seized the opportunity to talk about her family with both hands. She'd wanted him to see Kevin as a real person with wonderful qualities, a family who loved him, and a daughter who needed him, not just as a dangerous mentally ill person should it turn out that Kevin was guilty of horrible acts. She'd wanted him to know that Kevin was more than just his illness and to soften him up to the possibility of treatment, instead of just punishment, for any crimes he'd committed.

And then she'd kissed him and that had seriously complicated everything, which had been plenty complicated enough to begin with. That one kiss from Jack Conroy had been more erotic than any full out sexual experience she'd ever had in her life. She still felt his arms around her and his lips on hers, and she wanted to weep because she wanted more, and the one thing she knew for sure in all this mess was that it could never happen again.

Chapter Eight

Tuesday, February 14ᵗʰ

"Go away, Becca." Kevin sat on the edge of his bed with his eyes closed and scrubbed his face with both hands, as if he hoped that when he opened them Becca would be gone.

Becca wasn't going anywhere. It was the third time he'd ordered her out, but his voice lacked heat and his tone lacked conviction. She was staying until visiting hours were over.

"You're looking good." And he was. He'd obviously had a shower and shaved. His clothes hung on him as a result of all the weight he'd lost, but they were clean and pressed.

"Go away, Becca." Kevin twisted his upper body so that his back was to her.

"Happy Valentine's Day." She dropped the big box of candy and the cards she'd brought with her on his lap. "The chocolate is from all of us. Open Cara's card first; she drew you a special picture."

At the mention of Cara's name, his eyes popped open in alarm. He jumped up, spilling everything on the floor, and ran to the doorway. He stuck his head out in the hallway and swiveled his neck in both directions. "She's not here, is she?"

"Of course not. She's too young. The hospital

wouldn't let her in even if Mom and Dad and I wanted to bring her for a visit. You know that."

He visibly relaxed and came back into the room. He left everything on the floor, right where it had landed, returned to his spot on the edge of the bed and turned his head to the wall.

"Go away, Becca," he said again, and made a shooing motion with his hand. "You're not safe."

"I'm not in any danger. No one here is going to bother me," she reassured him and bent down to pick up the box of chocolates and the cards.

"I'm the danger, Bec." His voice cracked. "*I* could hurt you."

She looked up and saw pure anguish in his eyes. She straightened, set the gift and cards on the night stand, and sat down next to him. He scooted away from her lickety split, all the way down to the foot of the bed.

"Why would you hurt me, Kevin? You've never done anything but protect me."

"I'm trying to protect you now, but you won't let me. Why won't you let me, Becca? Why are you making this so hard?" His eyes filled with tears.

"I'm here because I love you, Kevin," she said softly. "That's all."

"Do you know what year this is?" His voice rose, going high and shrill, and he waved his hands in the air, both sure signs of growing agitation. "Do you realize how old I am?"

"You're thirty-three," she said, baffled.

"Yes!" He said it triumphantly, as if she'd just answered the winning question on *Who Wants to Be a Millionaire*. "So will you go away now?"

He still wasn't making any sense. Well, it was

early yet. She knew that. Another few days on his anti-psychotic medication would make a huge difference. Right now, though, he was on the edge of losing it, and she didn't want to push him over the bend.

"Fine," she said. "I'll go. Enjoy the chocolates. I'll be back to see you again tomorrow."

"No," he shouted. "Not until January 1st. I'll be thirty-four then and everything will be all right. When I'm thirty-four, we'll be home free."

With a sigh she shrugged into her coat and picked up her purse. He'd seemed so much calmer when she'd first arrived that she'd gotten her hopes up. Prematurely, as it turned out. Fighting back tears, she headed for the door.

"Becca, wait."

She stopped and turned to look at him.

"What were you doing with that man yesterday? Do you know who he *is*? He's the *brother*. You need to stay away from him." He gave her his vintage big brother, do-as-I-say level gaze and then said, "Now go away."

Jack? Was he talking about Jack Conroy? In the middle of his meltdown yesterday, he'd somehow recognized Jack Conroy? Who still hadn't called. Not that she wanted him to—finally, she and Kevin were on the same page about something—but still. Why did men always say they were going to call when they had no intention of doing so?

"Becca," he said again as she pulled the door open. His voice was plaintive, the expression on his face little boy lost. "How much longer is it until January 1st?"

****

She didn't feel like cooking. She wasn't sure she

133

even felt like eating, but since she'd skipped lunch she probably ought not skip dinner, too. So what was it going to be, fast food or a bowl of cereal from her cupboard? Cereal, she decided.

She was halfway home when she remembered to turn her cell phone back on—she'd shut if off when she'd entered the hospital—and saw that she'd missed several calls: one from Eileen, one from her mother, and one from Jack. She punched the voice mail button and listened to her messages.

"No baby yet," Eileen said. "I'm going stir crazy. The kids are in Mother's Day Out on Thursday. Wanna meet for lunch? You can choose the place. Give me a call."

"Hi, honey." Her mother sounded the happiest Becca had heard her in weeks. "I've been meaning to tell you that the children's choir is singing in church this Sunday. Cara wants you to come." She didn't do church, and now she was going to sit in a pew two Sundays in a row? She'd better watch out or somebody was going to start hounding her to pledge.

"I hope you like Chinese food because I'm going to be at your place a little after seven with carry out."

Seven was—she looked at her car clock—a mere three minutes away. And wasn't that typical of Jack Conroy, the high handed and presumptuous telling instead of asking. And yet, against all reason, her heart lifted. Dinner problem solved. She loved Chinese food. He'd called.

She rang Eileen and set up lunch for Thursday, at Kilkenney's, since it was her choice. Then she touched base with her mother and assured her that she wouldn't miss seeing Cara and the children's choir on Sunday for anything. By the time she disconnected from the second call, she was turning onto her street. She'd no more than parked in the driveway when Jack's Jeep pulled in behind her.

Her heart tripped when he stepped out of his car and headed toward her. The memory of that kiss surfaced, and she felt flushed all over again. In a few long-legged strides, he was beside her. He took the briefcase out of her hand, held up the large paper bag from which emanated the spicy, mouthwatering scent of Chinese food, said "Let's get you fed," leaned down, and dropped a quick kiss on her lips like it was something he did every night.

The longing that rose up in her almost stopped her in her tracks. Someone to come home to at night. Someone who came home to her. The kiss goodbye in the morning, the welcome home kiss in the evening. The shared meals. Two kids and a dog. She tripped on the front step and jarred herself out of the fantasy. It was a child's fantasy, anyway. No kids for her. She'd made that painful decision when she'd learned that schizophrenia was an inherited illness. And no kids probably meant no husband, another painful lesson. Even if Fate waved a magic wand and a cure for schizophrenia was discovered tomorrow, and all her dreams came true, Jack Conroy was the one man on the planet who was totally off limits to her. Kevin was right. She needed to stay away from him. As soon as Kevin was in the clear she'd start backing away from Jack.

She flipped on lights as she went through the living room and into the kitchen. She got out plates and glasses, and fixed them something to drink while Jack dished out the food. Earlier she'd thought she was too tired to eat, but now she realized she was hungry enough to eat a horse and chase the rider.

She sat and started in on the sesame chicken. Delicious. So was the sweet and sour pork, she discovered a few minutes later, and the broccoli beef with cashews.

"Yum, yum," she said.

"Yeah," he said, his gaze fastened on her lips. "Yum, yum."

And just like that, the kiss was there between them. Her stomach fluttered and her pulse jumped and she looked away.

"How's your brother?" Jack asked.

"A little better. What happened with the stalker yesterday? I didn't read about it in the *Tulsa World* this morning so I'm assuming he wasn't our guy."

"You assume right. He was an ex-husband in violation of a protective order; third time so we got to dress him in orange and put him up in the city jail." He smiled in satisfaction, and then his expression turned serious. He put down his fork, propped his elbows on the table, and leaned forward.

"Speaking of protective orders, did you know that Stan Marshall beat up his last girl friend when she broke up with him?"

"You're kidding." To say she was shocked was the understatement of the millennium. She'd never seen even a hint of that in him. Appetite gone, she pushed her plate away. How could she not have known Stan was violent? That shook her up more than anything— the fact that she hadn't perceived the rage in a man she'd dated for several months. She'd always believed she had sort of a sixth sense about potential violence, and that belief had been central to her feelings of safety and security.

"Not kidding. He broke two of her ribs. If it makes you feel any better, she says she didn't have a clue that he even had a temper until his fist connected with her ribcage."

The visual image of that had her stomach churning. The smell of soy sauce and sweet and sour was making her nauseated. She got up and began to put the food away.

"Did he ever get mean like that with you?" There was a hard edge to his voice that captured her attention. She turned to face him.

"Never. Trust me, I'd have pressed charges, and it would be a matter of public record."

"Glad to hear that." His solemn gaze held hers for a long minute, and then his lips quirked in a half smile. "Saves me from having to pound his face in."

She knew she should be appalled by the banked aggression, and instead a thrill of delight snaked through her. Disgusted with herself, she squelched it.

"It's not your job to pound faces on my behalf." God, did she sound prissy or what? "But thanks anyway," she added.

"I have no use for men who bully women and kids," he said softly. "The pounding would be pure pleasure."

For a minute he looked as if he might be going to say more, but then he gave a slight shake of his head, stood and began carrying dishes to the sink. He rinsed the plates and utensils and handed them to her to put in the dishwasher. After the dishwasher was loaded, she poured them each a cup of coffee.

"Thanks for dinner," she said, walking into the living room. "I was going to settle for a bowl of Frosted Flakes." One cup of coffee and she was hustling him out the door. There would be no repeats on the kissing.

He put a hand on her shoulder and massaged the tight muscles at the base of her neck. It felt so good she almost whimpered. He sat on the sofa, took a sip of coffee, and then set his cup on the end table.

"Have a seat." He patted the cushion next to him, took her cup and placed it on the end table next to his. "Turn around. I'll give you a back rub before I go."

He gathered her hair up in both hands and draped it across her shoulder. He settled his hands on either side of her neck began a slow massage. Her chin dropped to her chest as his fingers worked their magic, kneading, rubbing, soothing, easing the tension in her neck and back. Little by little her mind slowed and her body relaxed.

"Feels good," she murmured. It felt wonderful. She drifted as his thumbs inched up the sides of her spine.

"See a bunch of clients today?"

"Mmm." His voice seemed to be coming from a long way away.

"Visited your brother. Reassured your mom, I'll bet, and your niece."

"Mmm." The cushions on the sofa were so soft; she snuggled in deeper. Was she lying down?

"You're so busy taking care of other people," he whispered against her ear. "Who takes care of you?"

"Lots of people," she mumbled.

"Name one," he challenged, his voice smooth and rough at the same time, like water flowing through gravel.

"You." She sighed. Had she said that out loud? His hands rubbed slow circles on her back, over to her ribcage, up to her shoulders, down to the small of her back. Nothing in her life had ever felt so good. She thought she might be dreaming.

Had she said him? Her voice had been so soft and low, a bare whisper, that he couldn't be sure, but his chest swelled with tenderness, and hope. Because he wanted to be that man for her. He wanted to be the man who took care of her, who lightened her load, who stood between her and all the bad things in the world.

Jack continued to stroke her even after he was pretty sure she'd fallen asleep. The soft, vulnerable nape of her neck fascinated him. The inward curve of her waist pleased him. The flare of her hips called to him. He slid both hands back to her shoulders, round and firm and seemingly too narrow for the weight of all she carried. And weren't appearances deceiving? Because Rebecca Bennett was the strongest woman he knew.

And she needed him.

****

Wednesday, February 15th

At least she wasn't old like the last one. He guessed this one to be in her early thirties; pretty close to his own age. Short and plump with a round, plain face dotted with freckles and a shy smile, she looked like the all American girl next door. Her appearance was deceiving, of course.

All he had to do now was wait. She'd turned her dachshund puppy into the back yard to do its nightly business. She'd open the door to call it back inside in five minutes. He'd slipped a thin rope through the collar and tied the dog to the grill on her patio. She'd see him when she opened the door and she'd have to leave the safety of the house to get her pet.

He was glad he'd had the idea of tying the dog up. He still felt bad about the cats and dogs he'd killed when he was a kid. He'd really been messed up back then. He wasn't sure he could hurt an animal now. Animals weren't like people. They weren't evil. Only people were evil.

He'd been thinking about the note he'd left Becca. That might not have been a smart move on his part. He thought she was good, but one thing he'd learned over the last six weeks was that he wasn't a very good judge. Almost all of the women God had picked for punishment had surprised him. So he had to stay open to the possibility that he was wrong about Becca, too.

If she truly understood, she would appreciate his thoughtfulness, and that note would stay between the two of them. If, however, she turned that note over to the police knowing they were trying to stop him from fulfilling his mission, he'd know the truth about her. He'd know that she was just another Mary.

****

Becca could not get to sleep. Her mind was like a hyperactive gerbil in an exercise wheel, running in circles, going over and over the same thoughts. By this time tomorrow, she'd know if Kevin had raped and killed those women. If a new victim was discovered, then obviously Kevin hadn't done it; he was still locked up in the Psychiatric Unit. If no new victim was discovered, then Kevin would have to be the number one suspect.

She'd give it until the weekend and if the crime spree had come to a halt she knew what she had to do. She owed it to the victims and their families. She owed it to Kevin, because in his right mind Kevin wouldn't hurt anyone. In his right mind he'd beg to be locked up if that's what it took to keep him from hurting another person. So if there were no new developments before then, on Monday morning she'd do the right thing by everyone. She'd call Jack Conroy and turn her brother in.

She imagined the look of disgust and revulsion, the flat-out hatred, she'd see in Jack's eyes, and her stomach hurt so bad she could hardly breathe. She squeezed her eyes tightly shut against the tears that threatened. She had twenty years of tears stored inside, and she feared that if she ever started to cry she might not be able to stop.

She'd known from the beginning that she would come to this place. Whether Kevin were guilty or innocent, the outcome for her and Jack would be the same. Long before the moment he'd first said hello, they'd been racing to goodbye.

****

The shrill ring of the telephone jolted Jack out of an erotic dream in which Rebecca Bennett figured prominently. He knew before he answered it what he would hear. He grabbed the phone with one hand and his pants with the other.

"Our boy's been busy again," Sully said. "Next door neighbor called to report a dog howling. Livingston and Humphrey are on the scene. Half the neighborhood is gathered out front. They've got the area taped off. Livingston is keeping the curiosity seekers out and Humphreys has already started interviewing."

"Give me the address." Jack jotted down the street number and reached for his shoes. "On my way."

****

"The body of another woman was discovered shortly before midnight last night. Stay tuned. We'll be right back with more on this story."

Becca dropped her hairbrush and ran into the bedroom. She turned up the volume on the TV and sat on the foot of the bed, eyes glued to the screen. Elation filled her, rushing into every dry, dark, scared place in her like flood waters pouring onto parched soil, saturating her with relief and joy—Kevin was innocent!

Almost immediately her euphoria collapsed under the crushing weight of guilt. How could she, even for a second, be glad that another woman had been brutally murdered? What kind of monster had she become, that she celebrated someone else's awful misfortune? Shame scorched her cheeks and bowed her head.

"Marlene Johnson called 9-1-1 at eleven thirty-five last night," said the perfectly made up, appropriately solemn, blonde reporter. "Tell us about it, Mrs. Johnson."

The camera focused on an overweight woman with thinning gray hair who leaned heavily on a walker and panted as if she'd recently overexerted herself.

"The little dog woke me up, howling. Poor thing just howled and howled. It was the most pitiful sound." She dabbed at her eyes with a wadded up tissue. "After a bit I called Heather, but she didn't answer. When the answering machine came on, I knew something was terrible wrong because the lights were still on inside her place, but she didn't pick up the phone, and she didn't bring the puppy inside. I thought maybe she'd fallen in the tub—that happened to my granddaughter a year or so ago, knocked herself clean out—or she'd taken real bad sick. So I called for the police to come." A fresh wave of tears coursed down her lined face.

"Next thing I knew, the police car was in her driveway with the lights flashing, and a nice young officer was knocking on my door. Him and his partner had found Heather out back. The little dog was sitting beside her dead body, howling." She averted her face as she sobbed.

Becca sat straight up as the smiling freckled face of a young woman filled the screen. "This is Heather McCall. Her parents, Jim and Carol McCall, are offering a substantial reward for any information that leads to the arrest of their daughter's murderer. If you know anything, call Crime Stoppers at 555-1234."

Chills crawled down Becca's spine and over her arms. She knew that woman. Well, she didn't *know* her, know her, but she'd seen her recently. She searched her memory trying to place when and where but came up empty. She wasn't a client or a neighbor. She shook her head in frustration. Where had she seen her?

She got up, shut the TV off, returned to the bathroom, and finished getting ready for the day. She was halfway to her office when she abruptly changed direction. She had group this evening and wouldn't be able to visit Kevin then, but her first appointment wasn't until late morning. She could go now.

She caught him at the tail end of breakfast. For the first time he looked glad to see her. His face broke out in a big smile, and he scooted away from the table, hurried to her, and caught her up in a bear hug, twirled her around.

"How's my favorite sister?" It was a long-standing joke and she laughed.

"Good. How's my favorite brother?" She leaned back to look at him. He had color in his cheeks and light in his eyes. How in the world had she ever thought he might have killed someone?

"Ready to get out of this place, but don't worry, I'll stay until the doc thinks I'm good to go." His smile dimmed. "I was pretty far out there this time."

"You want to tell me about it?"

"Sure." He caught her hand in his and started walking to his room. "Ever since I can remember, I've been scared I'd turn out like Dad. He was thirty-three when he killed that little girl, and the closer I came to that age the more scared I got. So I decided I'd leave and stay gone for my thirty-third year. That way, if I morphed into Dad, Cara would be safe." He shrugged. "Made sense at the time."

"Oh, Kevin, you could never be like Dad." Tears stung her eyes as she realized she'd worried about the same thing for him. She couldn't begin to imagine the torment he'd lived with.

"Same illness. Same voices."

"But you'd never hurt Cara," she protested. "You adore her, and you're one of the most loving fathers I've ever seen."

"Dad loved you, too," he said, pushing through the door to his room, "and we both know what almost happened." He stopped just inside the door and turned a level gaze on her. "We've never talked about it, but we know, don't we?"

"Yes," she whispered, light headed and feeling as if her knees were going to give out on her any minute. She stumbled to the bed and dropped onto it, her heart galloping in her chest like a runaway horse.

"Which reminds me." His eyes narrowed. "What were you doing with Jack Conroy the other day? Do you know who he is? Does he know who you are?"

"He's Megan Conroy's older brother. And no, he doesn't know who I am. He asked me to work with several women who are victims of the same rapist, who has now graduated to murder. I agreed."

"Gee," he muttered, "and everyone thinks I'm the crazy one. Have you lost your mind?"

"What's the matter?" She grinned at him. "Afraid of a little competition?"

"Right. Don't even think about horning in on my occupational therapy group. Your pot holders for sure would turn out better than mine."

And just like that they were laughing, the way they'd laughed together since they were kids. For the first time in weeks, she felt like everything was going to be okay. Her brother was safe. He had not followed in their father's footsteps. He hadn't hurt anyone. He was not going to prison. Her family was not going to be at the center of another scandal.

And maybe, just maybe, if her luck held, Jack Conroy would only know her for who she was now, Rebecca Bennett, and never who she had been, who she was all those years ago as little Becky Harrison, daughter of Millard Harrison, the girl in whose stead his sister had been murdered.

****

"I guess you heard about poor Heather," Georgie

said as they restacked the plastic chairs after group. "I feel so bad for Carol and Jim. I don't know how people without faith get through a tragedy like this." Her eyes filled with tears. "That girl was good as gold. You could probably tell that from meeting her just the one time. The whole church is going to feel her loss."

It struck Becca then, with the force of a fist to the solar plexus, where she'd seen Heather McCall: She and her mother had sat in the seats next to Becca last Sunday at Church of the Lamb.

"Oh, my God." The tremors started in her abdomen and radiated outward all the way to her hands and feet. She groped for the table to steady herself with one hand and pressed the other over her stomach, which roiled with nausea. "I just put it together. I knew she looked familiar."

Georgie began to cry in earnest. Her own eyes stinging, Becca wrapped her arms around Georgie and the two women held each other tightly. Finally Georgie's sobbing subsided.

"This world is a hard place," Georgie said. Becca nodded. Silently, they put on their coats and gathered their purses and walked out together.

"See you next week." Becca gave Georgie one last hug before they got into their separate cars. She'd just turned out onto Twenty-First Street when her cell phone rang. It was Jack.

"You home yet?"

"Headed that way. I'm falling into bed as soon as I get there." Not only was she physically and emotionally exhausted, but it was time for her to start pulling away from Jack Conroy.

"I'll be there in ten minutes. Considering the fact

that our psycho killer is a secret admirer of yours, I got some things to make your place a little more secure. It won't take long and you'll sleep safer." He hung up before she could answer.

Not that she would have argued. The words "secret admirer" had cut through her like an arctic wind and set off a spasm of shivering so severe that her teeth were chattering. Somehow she'd managed not to think about the sinister implications of Kevin's innocence. She'd drawn the attention of a cold-blooded murderer. Who knew where she lived. Who could be hiding at the side of her house right now, or watching her from down the street. Who could even be, oh God, inside her house.

She pulled into her driveway and sat inside her locked car, waiting for Jack to get there. She peered into the shadows all around her and scanned for unfamiliar cars. Her heart pounded in her chest like a jackhammer, and her hands, cold and clammy, shook so badly it took her several tries to get the key out of the ignition. She was going to start leaving the porch light on.

When Jack pulled up behind her and got out of the Jeep, she felt faint with relief. She'd never been so glad to see anyone in her life. Her fingers fumbled with the door handle, and when she stood she had to lean against the side of the car for a minute until the dizziness passed.

As he had several nights ago, Jack dropped a casual kiss on her lips, took her briefcase, and walked with her to the house.

"I know you're tired, so I'll get the basics done as quickly as I can." He followed her in, set down her briefcase and his toolbox, and cast his burning blue gaze her way. "If you change your mind about the security system, let me know."

"I changed my mind."

"Good." He smiled. "I'll get Doug out here first thing in the morning. Seven too early for you?"

"Seven will be fine. Thank you. And thank you for coming over tonight." Inexplicably, she was on the verge of tears. Quickly she turned away. She was not a crier, damn it. But he was taking care of her again, and it touched her heart in a way that nothing else could.

"Want something to drink? Coffee? Pop?"

"Coffee would be great."

She escaped into the kitchen. It was turning out to be a lot harder to distance herself from Jack Conroy than she'd thought it would be. Just by being who he was, he was meeting needs she hadn't even known she had. He wouldn't be so darn nice to her if he knew who she was, she reminded herself.

When the coffee finished brewing, she poured some into a mug for him and carried it into the living room. He'd already cut a hole in her door and was fitting in a double keyed deadbolt lock. The muscles in his arms and shoulders flexed as he tightened the screws that held it in place. She wanted to smooth her hand over those muscles just for the pleasure of it, and maybe to lighten some of the burdens he carried on that broad back. *He's off limits*, she told herself again, and cleared her throat to get his attention.

"Thanks." He reached for the mug and gave her a bone melting smile. "One lock down, one to go. Then I'll secure the windows and be out of your way." He took several deep swallows and set the mug down on an end table, lifted the toolbox, and carried it to the back door.

"Take your time. I really appreciate what you're doing for me." That was the understatement of the millennium. If he hadn't shown up, she wasn't sure she could even have gotten out of the car, never mind getting any sleep tonight. Partly because of the new locks and mostly, she feared, because of his presence, she'd quit shaking, and she no longer felt as cold as if she'd been staked to an ice floe.

After the second lock was installed, he drilled holes in her window sashes and inserted nails. "The windows can't be raised from the outside as long as the nails are in here," he explained. "This ought to hold you until morning."

When the windows had all been secured, he replaced his tools in the box, finished off his coffee, and pulled his coat on. Becca walked him to the door.

She saw the kiss coming but couldn't move away. He slanted his head, sealed his lips over hers, and just that quickly she was drowning in sensation. Every nerve ending in her body was firing with pleasure. His tongue swirled against hers, tasting of coffee and cravings. He groaned, and the sound vibrated through her. Somehow she was closer, but still not close enough even though she pressed against him, breasts to chest and all the way down to their thighs. Her arms twined around the thick column of his neck, and her fingers tangled in his hair.

His hand held her head firmly in place while he devoured her. She melted under his heat, turning into liquid want, and had she not been holding onto him her legs might have given way.

"Invite me back in or send me away," he whispered

against her lips.

****

She'd called the cops? The pain of her betrayal sliced through him like the sharp blade of a knife. Obviously he'd been very wrong about Becca. He watched her practically having sex with the man who was hunting him.

She wouldn't get away with this. She deserved to be punished. And he had earned the right to punish her. He stroked his knife, every bit as sharp as her betrayal, and vowed she'd feel the sharp edge of it. Soon.

Chapter Nine

Thursday, February 16th

Jack stood rooted in place, holding his breath, and waited for Becca to let him know if they'd continue this inside or stop right here. If sheer force of desire on his part could compel the outcome, they'd be naked in her bed right now. But he said nothing, did nothing; it had to be her decision.

Her brown-eyed gaze, slightly out of focus, held him captive. Her chest rose and fell rapidly, air gusting from her parted lips in quick erratic puffs. Her hands gripped his shoulders and her thighs, pressing against his, trembled.

Thunder boomed overhead and the skies opened, sending down sheets of rain as the storm the weather forecasters had been predicting all day broke loose. The wind howled and pushed hard against his back. He stood firm against it. He wasn't moving from this spot until Becca told him which way to go.

Becca knew she'd be making a big mistake to ask Jack back inside. Because she wouldn't just be inviting him into her house, she'd be inviting him into her bed, and they both knew it. She was paralyzed with indecision because the argument for and the argument against was the same: she liked Jack Conroy. She pretty much liked everything about him. His dogged determination and his sense of humor. His quick mind and the way he smelled. His big hands, both strong and safe. The way he took charge, and the way he relinquished control. Like right now. What happened next was strictly her call.

She was supposed to be pulling away from him, for God's sake, and the two of them getting horizontal together certainly wouldn't further that cause. But the thing was, she'd led such a careful life, a half life really, and before she returned to it she wanted this one thing, just for her. She'd never felt this way before, so exhilaratingly alive, and she wanted to hold onto it for a little bit longer. She wanted to spend a whole evening in the vivid Technicolor world that she experienced when she was with Jack Conroy before she went back to the pale, muted shades of her own.

The familiar voice of caution whispered in her ear that she'd regret it, probably in a matter of mere hours, if she succumbed to the wild desire he aroused in her. A different voice, one that urged her to live and that she'd spent her whole life trying to silence, shouted that she'd be sorry for the rest of her life if she didn't.

She slid her palms down his arms to his hands and took them in hers, linking their fingers. Smiling, she took a step backward and whispered, "Come with me."

His eyes darkened to a cerulean blue as he followed her. Stopping only long enough to lock the new dead bolt behind them and hang his damp jacket on the coat rack, she led him down the hall and into her bedroom. She backed all the way to the edge of the bed before she let go of his hands and began to undo the buttons of her blouse.

He brushed her fingers away and replaced them

with his. "Let me," he murmured. "I've imagined this a thousand times. Maybe more."

His blue eyes burned flame bright as his fingers released one button and then another. The backs of his knuckles stroked her bare skin as he worked his way from collar to hem and left a trail of shivering desire in their wake. Her blouse fell open, and he slipped his cool hands inside and covered her breasts at the same time his hot mouth came down on hers.

Yes. This was what she wanted, what she craved. All this feeling. All this heat. All this glorious sensation. Her arms circled his waist; her hands slid up his back and then down to tug his shirt out of the waistband of his jeans before gliding underneath it. His skin was smooth, the muscles underneath hard. She was dizzy with the feel of him, the taste of him.

Jack swirled his tongue over Becca's, drawing the taste of her into his mouth. He found the front clasp of her bra and freed her breasts from the black lace, caressed her nipples with his thumbs and felt them pebble, deepened the kiss and swallowed her gasps of pleasure.

Too many clothes. His hands shook as he pushed her blouse and the straps of her bra over her shoulders and let both garments drop to the floor. Apparently she had the same thought because she quickly undid the buttons on his shirt and pulled it off him. The instant his shirt was out of the way he hugged her to him, breast to chest, bare skin on bare skin. The sensation was exquisite, everything he'd imagined, and still not enough. He peeled her slacks and panties off and then stripped away his jeans and briefs with one swift jerk. He wanted to feel all of her, every inch of her, with nothing between them but want.

Dropping one knee onto the edge of the bed, he lowered her to the mattress and then followed her down. He caught himself on one elbow and lifted his head to look at her. She gleamed like alabaster in the light from the hallway. He'd never seen anything more beautiful in his life.

He traced the curve of her cheek and the line of her jaw with his fingertips, stroked a path to the hollow of her throat and rested there briefly before moving lower. He circled one breast and then the other, drew a line to her navel. He traveled the same pathway with his tongue and kept going, all the way to that sweet spot between her legs. The sound of her ragged breathing and soft moans was as sweet to his ear as the taste of her was on his tongue, and both sent his own need spiraling upward.

Her hands fisted in his hair as she convulsed beneath his mouth. Rain pounded against the windowpanes, the wind screeched through the trees, and a boom of thunder shook the house, but the storm outside was nothing compared to the one raging inside him. Air billowed in his lungs, gusting out in blasts. Electricity crackled along his nerve endings, raising goose bumps. Lightning flashed in his veins and thunder rolled in his chest as he moved back up her body, leaving a meandering trail of wet kisses from her stomach to her breasts and up to her throat.

Nothing in her life had ever felt so good, or so right, as the weight of Jack Conroy on top of her. He made love the way he did everything—thoroughly, intensely, with care and attention to detail. Becca smiled up at him as he framed her face with his hands.

He was looking at her like she was the cherished center of his universe, and she knew that if she lived to be a hundred and twenty she'd never forget this one magic night with him. She caressed his cheek, rough as a cat's tongue under her palm, clasped his hips with her thighs, and urged him to come inside her with the pressure of her heels against his bare buttocks.

"More," she whispered against his lips, and when he filled her she got more. More pleasure than she'd imagined possible. More feelings than she'd thought she could hold. More aliveness than she'd thought her body could contain. She was stunned at the discovery that when her senses were saturated with him, with the taste, feel, and scent of him, she felt more like herself than ever before.

She waltzed with him in the mating dance that was as old as the human race and as miraculous as each new birth, slowly at first and then faster and faster, until he spun her all the way out of herself.

In the quiet after the storm, Jack wrapped both arms around Becca and tucked her into his side. She curled against him with her head on his chest, right over his heart, right where he wanted her, right where she belonged.

****

Friday, February 17th

Becca awoke to the low rumbling of male voices coming from the other room. One of those voices belonged to Jack. She didn't recognize the other one.

She got out of bed and threw on a pair of jeans and an old University of Oklahoma sweatshirt, brushed her teeth, washed her face, finger combed her hair, and went out to investigate.

155

"Becca." Jack greeted her with a slow, private smile and then turned to the man standing by the front door. "Doug, this is Rebecca Bennett. Becca, Doug Horacek, from Horacek Home Security Systems."

"Pleased to meet you, Mr. Horacek." Becca nodded at the red-haired, brown-eyed giant who, in his younger days, had doubtless been the star on some football coach's offensive line. "Thanks for fitting me in on such short notice."

"Doug, and it's no problem." His voice was as rough as a pitted gravel road. "I'll have you fixed up here in a couple of hours. Then I'll head on over to your office and get you taken care of there, too."

"I appreciate it."

"Why don't you finish getting ready, and I'll take you out for breakfast," Jack suggested. He moved several steps closer to her, winked, and added in a low voice, "I seem to have worked up a pretty good appetite."

Before she could respond, his cell phone buzzed. He listened for half a minute, said, "Good work. I'll be there in ten," and pocketed the phone.

"Livingston found a witness. I'll have to take a rain check on breakfast." He kissed her, hard and fast, grabbed his jacket, and strode out the door, taking all the air in the room out with him.

Becca watched him until he was out of sight and struggled to breathe around the emptiness that sat heavy as a concrete block in the middle of her chest. Her one night of mind blowing, soul stirring, every molecule in her body celebrating the magic with Jack Conroy was now officially over.

She'd known going into it that this morning would

come, and he would leave, and that would be that. She'd anticipated feeling blah, maybe even a little sad. But she'd never imagined this deep, hollow-as-a-drum ache.

****

Finally, a break. Jack felt it, the hum just beneath the surface of his skin that he always got when things started happening on a case.

The boy, Clark Lydell, was fifteen years old and scared. He'd sneaked out his bedroom window Wednesday night and climbed the big oak tree in his back yard to think, he'd said. To smoke cigarettes, or maybe pot, was more likely in Jack's opinion. The teenager had hesitated and slid a nervous glance at his dad before he'd settled on the word "think." His father had caught it, too, and started to question his son, but Jack had interrupted. He didn't care if the kid had been up there shooting heroin, he wanted to know what he'd seen.

A big white guy—well, not tall, but built—wearing all black, had cut through their yard. He'd been carrying a wad of black cloth—probably the ski mask, Jack thought—in his left hand. He'd walked right under the oak tree and around the side of the house. A small dog was howling a couple of blocks away. Clark had gotten himself inside the house as soon as the man had disappeared from sight, and gone straight to the living room window to look out. He'd seen a dark—black or navy blue, he was pretty sure black—2006 Chrysler LeBaron, two door, no headlights, driving away, slowly. The headlights hadn't come on until after he turned the corner. The car had no dents, no scrapes, no bumper stickers, nothing dangling from the rear view mirror. The car itself had been clean, shiny as a new quarter, but thick mud had streaked the license plate, and he hadn't been able to get the number. Thank God for the American adolescent male's fascination with cars. With the detailed description of the LeBaron, the kid had given him his first solid lead.

"Do you think you'd recognize the man if you saw him again?" Jack had asked.

"Absolutely," had come the confident answer.

Now they were searching through vehicle registration records, tracking down all the dark 2006 Chrysler LeBarons in Tulsa County.

****

Sunday, February 19th

Becca sat wedged between her mother and Kevin. Charles Bennett had led them all the way to the front of the sanctuary, to the third pew, directly behind the rows occupied by the members of the children's choir.

Cara was radiant. She hadn't quit grinning since Kevin had come home yesterday. She was twisted around in her seat right now, beaming a high wattage smile at her dad. Kevin beamed right back.

"Isn't she the cutest kid in the world?" he asked Becca.

"And the smartest," Becca agreed. She looked from Kevin to Cara, to Marie, and then Charles. They were, each one, precious to her. Her heart was full to bursting with love for them. Her family. There was nothing she wouldn't do for them. If only... No, she wouldn't think about Jack. Not now. Not when they were all together again.

The service began as Reverent Koeing issued the Call to Worship. Kevin motioned to Cara to turn around in her seat and face the front which, with a giggle and after blowing him a kiss, she did.

Becca looked at her bulletin. She'd grown up in this church, and even after a twelve-year absence, the order of the worship service was as familiar to her as her own face in the mirror: Call to Worship, Hymn of Praise, Confession of Sin, Declaration of Pardon, Gloria Patri, Prayer of Illumination, Reading of Scripture, Hymn of Praise, Sermon, Apostles' Creed, Hymn, Concerns of the Church (including announcements, prayer requests, Ritual of Friendship and Passing of the Peace), Offering, Anthem, Doxology, Prayer of Thanksgiving, the Lord's Prayer, Closing Hymn, Charge and Benediction. She found the first song in the hymnal and shared the book with Kevin, just like when they were kids.

After the Scripture readings, the children's choir filed to the front of the sanctuary and turned to face the congregation. Cara waved at Kevin and then turned her gaze to Leslie Peron, the choir director. Throughout the song her eyes flickered back to her dad, as if to make sure he was still there, and at the song's conclusion she grinned broadly at him. Becca fervently hoped that Kevin would see how much his daughter loved and needed him and keep the vow he'd made yesterday when she'd picked him up at the hospital—to never again quit taking his medication. "In fact, if I go first, you slip a bottle of Seroquel into the casket with me," he'd joked.

"And a script for unlimited refills," she'd teased.

Becca tried to keep her mind focused on the sermon, but it kept returning to Jack. She'd had one brief conversation with him on Friday evening when he'd called to make sure that her alarm systems were up and running. "Good," he'd said. "Use them."

The sound of his voice had made her stomach flutter and her skin tingle and her mouth go dry. Just thinking about him now was making her heart beat faster and the whole rest of her body ache for his touch. She sighed. How had she let herself fall so hard for the one man on the planet she couldn't have?

She'd get over him, she told herself. She'd grieved losses and forfeited dreams enough times in her life to know that a person could, indeed, accept the unbearable and go on.

She was roused from her reverie when her mother handed her the Ritual of Friendship pad. She passed it on to Kevin without signing it and ignored the look of disapproval aimed her way. Her mother could frown all she wanted; Becca wasn't caving. She did not need one of the deacons calling on her and encouraging her to reactivate her membership. She'd already fielded an invitation to visit Church of the Lamb again from a woman who'd gotten her name off the fellowship sheet that she'd unthinkingly signed last week.

The back of her neck prickled as she remembered reading Heather McCall's name on that Fellowship sheet and meeting her at the end of the service. She shook off the unease that crawled up her spine at the recollection and smiled at Cara as the children's choir sang the anthem that accompanied the offering.

****

The first thing Jack had done on Friday after leaving Clark Lydell was find out the makes and models of the cars owned by the men on the list he and Becca had made a week ago. Not a single damn match.

He'd been so certain that the car would lead him to one of those men. Time to get back to Becca and mine her memory again. Clearly she'd missed someone.

If that someone was a client, or connected to a client, he was shielded by her professional ethic of confidentiality. Did he have enough to convince a judge to issue a subpoena for her files? He scrubbed his face with both hands. Probably not, but he'd try first thing in the morning anyway.

Every time he'd thought about her in the last two days, a wave of fear had whipped through him and driven him to work harder. Because as long as this guy was free, Becca's life was in danger. Keeping her alive had become a very personal mission. There was nothing he could do to change the fact that he'd failed to protect Megan, but by God, he'd do whatever it took to keep Becca out of the hands of someone like Millard Harrison.

He'd hit it hard all weekend, and he'd run into dead end after dead end. There was nothing more he could do right now except work the connection of the killer to Becca. He punched in her cell phone number. Just when he thought it was going into voice mail she answered.

"I need to go over some things with you," he said. "Half an hour okay?"

"Make it forty-five minutes."

Rejuvenated by the prospect of seeing her, he surged to his feet, grabbed his jacket and his keys, and headed out the door. First stop: Goldie's, for two of the best hamburgers in town and fries. He laughed to himself. He needed to keep her strength up for what he had in mind once the brainstorming session was over.

****

Even though it had warmed up, it would get cold again, and Becca had bagged up all the winter clothes she no longer wore and brought them to the Day Center for the Homeless. She'd stopped at Target on the way to purchase several packages each of socks and underwear and a couple of decks of cards. She was so grateful that Kevin had survived his time on the street, and she knew it was in no small part a result of the day center; he'd said they'd kept him in thick, dry socks and warm gloves, and several times had provided clean jeans and once a sweatshirt.

"Hey, Darlene," she called out as she edged her way through the door, lugging two black plastic bags in with her. "Where do you want me to put these clothes?"

"Stick them in the office for now. I'll get to them when I get to them." The older woman, looking harried, swiped at a gray curl that had fallen over one eye. "Sorry. I don't mean to sound so grumpy. David didn't show up, and he didn't bother to call, either; I've been here by myself all afternoon. Here, let me give you a hand." She grabbed one of the bags and heaved it over her shoulder.

"Thanks. That's not like David. I hope he's okay." Becca deposited her bag next to the one Darlene had set down just inside the office door. The tiny space was packed to the gills.

"That boy has been moody as all get out for several weeks; probably has girl trouble." She huffed out a deep breath and backed out of the office. "I'm going to just shut this door and pretend I don't know all this is in here. Let someone else worry about it."

"I'll be in on Saturday. If it's still here, I'll do it then." She glanced at her watch. Jack was going to be at her house in ten minutes. She'd better get a move on.

She reminded herself that she had to keep it all business from here on out with Jack, but that reminder did not have the desired effect. Her traitorous heart continued to race like a runaway thoroughbred, her stomach went on fluttering, and her skin persisted in tingling, all from the anticipation of seeing him again. Before she started the car she flipped down the visor and looked at herself critically in the mirror. Calling herself all kinds of fool she applied fresh lipstick and added some blush to her cheeks.

****

Jack pulled up to the curb in front of Becca's duplex and noted that her car was not in the driveway. He'd already filched a couple of French fries, and if she didn't show up soon, he was going to filch a few more. He grabbed the sack of food, walked to the porch, and sat down on the top step.

The sun was a bright orange ball, dropping toward the tree tops. The indigo sky was streaked with red and purple, highlighted in places with lavender. Lights came on across the street and the windows glowed, pale yellow rectangles of warmth and welcome. Two preadolescent boys zigzagged down the street on skateboards and a middle-aged woman walking a pair of white toy poodles waved at him as she passed by.

The air was chilly but not cold. The sound of voices and laughter drifted to him from down the block, and the bare branches of the trees rustled in the breeze. A sharp memory of sitting in a porch swing, side by side with his grandfather, and watching the sun set, bobbed on the surface of his mind like a blessing.

"A man should never let himself get too busy to

kiss his wife, pet his dog, or watch the sun set," his grandfather had said.

How long had it been since he'd even noticed a sunset, never mind taken the time to watch it? He didn't have a wife any more; Britney had left after a year and a half, saying "I need a husband and you're married to your job, Jack. You won't even notice that I'm gone." And the sad truth was that he hadn't. He didn't have a dog, either, because he didn't have the time to take care of one. He lived in an apartment that remained as bare as it had been the day he'd moved in, almost eight years ago. He hadn't put up a single picture, hadn't replaced the sofa that Denise had taken, hadn't hung any curtains at the windows. Hell, he hadn't even unpacked all the boxes yet.

Sitting on Becca's front step, watching the sky turn as the day slid slowly into night, he wanted more. He was still absorbing that realization when Becca pulled into the driveway and got out of her car. The last dying rays of the sun gathered around her head like a halo. His throat constricted, and his heart swelled in his chest at the sight of her. A second awareness slammed into him with the force of a sledge hammer: the "more" he wanted was walking toward him with a tentative smile on her face.

For a few seconds he couldn't even breathe, let alone speak. Finally he managed, "Hey." His voice sounded hoarse even to his own ears.

"Hey yourself," she responded, stepping around him and fitting the key into the lock. "Come on in. I hope you haven't been waiting long."

All my life. "Just a few minutes." He grabbed the Goldie's sack and followed her inside. "I figured we might as well eat while we talk."

"Sounds like a plan." She punched the code into the alarm panel, hung her jacket on the coat rack, turned her head so that his kiss fell on her cheek, and then headed to the kitchen. "What can I get you to drink? Coffee? Pop? Iced tea?"

"Coffee sounds good." What the hell was going on? They'd made love three nights ago, he'd kissed and caressed every smooth inch of her body, and she was treating him as if he were a casual acquaintance. It had been the most fantastic experience of his life and now, boom, he was right back where he'd started—politely, but firmly, at arm's length.

"Who do you know who drives a Chrysler LeBaron?" he asked, transferring the food to the plates she'd put on the table.

"I don't know. What does one look like?"

"Like this." He pulled the brochure he'd picked up from the dealership out of his pocket and handed it to her. As a man, he was baffled by the female indifference to cars. As a cop, he'd anticipated it.

She studied the brochure and then shook her head. "I'm sorry. One car looks like another to me." She handed the brochure back to him. "Why do you ask?"

"Witness saw a man I'm pretty sure is our guy getting into one two blocks away from Heather McCall's house Wednesday night."

Her eyes clouded. "Did I tell you that I met her on the Sunday before she was killed?"

"Where?" Everything in him went on full alert.

"At Church of the Lamb. I went with my friend Georgie and her husband, Harold. Heather and her mother sat next to us." She shook her head. "She seemed like a very nice person."

"Start at the beginning and tell me everything." He pulled out a chair for her and then seated himself. Food forgotten, he listened as she recounted that morning, from the time she arrived in the parking lot to the time she drove away, and later that week, when Georgie had jogged her memory.

"I'm sure it was just a coincidence, my meeting her like that," she said when she'd finished.

"You were seated first?" Jack didn't believe in coincidences and neither did any other cop he knew. Coincidences did not solve crimes. No, there was something important here, hovering just beyond his grasp.

"Yes."

"Who knew you were going to be there?"

"Just Georgie and Harold."

"You'd never seen Heather McCall, spoken with her, or heard anything about her before that morning?"

"No."

"You first learned her name when she greeted you during the Passing of the Peace in church, when you heard it on the news or when your friend told you who she was?"

"I read her name on the fellowship sheet. I just didn't remember it or connect it with the woman who was murdered until Georgie reminded me."

"The fellowship sheet?" A buzz of adrenaline started in his chest and radiated outward.

"Lots of churches have them. They're called different things—fellowship sheets, Ritual of Friendship pads—but basically, it's a sign-in sheet. They say it's so you can greet the other people in your pew after the service by name, but really they want a record of which members are in attendance and the names of the guests so they know who to sic the deacons on." She snickered. "Tricky, but transparent, if you ask me. I mean, come on. You don't need to know someone's address or phone number to greet them after church. 'Hi, Miranda, 3312 South Maplewood, 742-8559,' " she said in a sing-song voice, " 'I'm Becca, 1424 South—' "

Bingo. The buzz morphed into a full scream.

"He's getting their names and addresses off the friendship pads." He shoved away from the table, reached for her, and then remembered that she'd turned away from him earlier. He'd get to the bottom of that soon.

"Here's how it's happening," he said. "I'll be back when I can get here. Then you'll tell me what's gone wrong between us, and I'll fix it. Lock up after me," he ordered as he went out the door.

Chapter Ten

Monday, February 20th

"Yes, Lillian Robinson was in church the Sunday before she was killed." The Reverend John Beardsley confirmed what Jack already knew. "She was a member for forty-eight years and rarely missed a service. All of us at Saint Ann's feel her loss keenly. It won't be the same around here without her."

"Where did she sit that last Sunday?" Jack asked.

"Down front, where she always sat. The fourth or fifth row." The older man frowned. "The fourth, I think."

Jack would bet his bank account that it had been the fifth row; the other victims had all been fifth row occupants. "Do you still have the attendance records for that day?"

"I believe we do. Martha," he said into the telephone receiver, "would you bring me the Our Church Family sheets for February 5th? Thanks." He hung up and rested his folded hands on the desk top, gazed out the window, and bowed his head briefly. Pink scalp shone through wispy white hair, making him appear painfully vulnerable.

"I'll want a copy of it."

The priest returned his attention to Jack, and nodded. "Anything I can do to help."

The church secretary, who looked to be years past the age of retirement, entered the room clutching a sheaf of papers. She set them in the middle of the desk and left the room quietly, closing the door behind her.

"They're not in any particular order," Father Beardsley apologized. "How about I take half and you take half?"

Jack nodded. Halfway through his stack he found Lillian Robinson's spidery signature. He studied the sheet. There'd been ten people in the row. Lillian had been the seventh from the end; so had Andrea Marple. Nancy Rojas, Juliet Crouch and Heather McCall had been fifth, Ann Wilson had been sixth.

Something niggled at his brain, circling just beyond his reach, taunting him. If he weren't so damned tired, he'd have grabbed hold of it by now. He suppressed a growl of frustration, handed the sheet to the priest, and followed him to the copier. He plucked the copy the machine spat out from the tray, folded it twice, and slid it into the pocket of his jacket. He'd compare it to the others and if nothing jumped out at him he'd grab a few hours of sleep.

Everywhere he turned, he was striking out. The lead that had looked so promising last night hadn't drawn an arrow pointing at the killer. Judge Coffee had denied his request for a subpoena of Becca's client list. And Becca was backing away from him at such a rapid clip that she'd be in the next county any minute now.

This evening he intended to corral Becca and pry some answers out of her if it took a crowbar and a pair of needle nose pliers.

****

When Becca turned the corner onto her street, she

wasn't surprised to see Jack's Jeep parked in front of her house. She had the urge to turn around and head the opposite direction, but she squelched it. She had many faults, but cowardice wasn't one of them. He thought there was a problem between them that he could fix and she loved that about him, his wanting to make things right, but her father had killed his sister and destroyed his family, and there was no fixing that. While she didn't plan to enlighten him as to the ugly truth, she did mean to make it plain that they had no future. Sucking in a deep breath, she pulled into the driveway and got out of the car.

All the lectures she'd given herself in the last three days weren't enough to keep her heart from lifting or her pulse from fluttering when she saw Jack sitting on the top step, a pizza box balanced on one knee, the other leg stretched out in front of him, a deceptively casual pose for a man who didn't have a casual bone in his body.

Faint lines of determination fanned out around his eyes as his gaze locked on her. He rose. Long, purposeful strides brought him toe to toe with her. She ordered herself to take a step back, out of kissing range, but her feet refused to obey. Her breath came faster, and she couldn't look away from those pale blue eyes that focused on her with unblinking intensity. Any second now he was going to see right through her camouflage, past the shields of a lifetime, clear down to her darkest secrets. That thought had her stumbling backward. He frowned and reached out with his free hand to steady her, then took her briefcase and turned toward the house.

"Here's the plan." He glanced at her over his

shoulder. "Food first, while it's still warm, then we'll talk. You on board with that?"

She nearly swooned with relief at the reprieve. "Sure."

She unlocked the front door, and he carried the pizza into the kitchen. He got out plates and napkins while she poured iced tea into glasses. The ease with which they worked together put a lump in her throat. She wished he were one of those men who expected a woman to wait on him; that was a turn off that ranked right up there with spitting on the sidewalk, and it'd make it so much easier to send him on his way. But no, Jack Conroy was a man who did his part, and more.

"You were a big help last night." He transferred a slice of pepperoni pizza to her plate. "He's getting their names off the friendship pads at churches. He's chosen all of his victims from the fifth row."

She nodded. She'd figured that out last night after he'd left so abruptly. "Same seat?"

"First thing I checked, but no." He'd polished off his first slice in three bites and now he reached for another. "Three were fifth from the end, one was sixth, and two were the seventh. You want to look at the sign-in sheets? Maybe you'll see something I missed."

She nodded, and he reached into his pocket, pulled out several folded sheets, and handed them to her. Just seeing their names made her sad. They'd signed these sheets only days before they'd been brutally raped and murdered. Every day she was witness to the fact that life was unpredictable and death was capricious, and she knew better than most that life didn't come with any guarantees, that violence could be random as well as purposeful, that "fair" was an abstract concept and not reality. Still, she looked at the names and she wanted to weep, for these women and for all those who loved them, for the little boy who'd grown up to be a killer and for all those who loved him.

She blinked and looked away, took a sip of tea and moved her plate to one side, pulled the papers closer and arranged them in two rows of three, precisely placed. When she felt in control again, she studied the sheets. She counted down from the top and up from the bottom. She eliminated the names obviously written by a child and counted again. She skipped those who'd put a check mark in the "guest" column. She shook her head and started to stack the sheets when it hit her. She separated them again and recounted.

"Each victim was either the fifth person in from the outside of the pew or, if that position was occupied by a man, the fifth woman in the pew. Look." She shoved the pages at Jack.

He quickly scanned the sheets and then flashed a grin that made her stomach quiver and her heart stutter. Tears threatened as she realized this would probably be the last time he'd look at her and toss an easy, open grin her way. He stuffed the papers back into his pocket.

"Any idea what the significance of the number five might be?"

"None whatsoever. Sorry. I'm guessing that it's symbolic of something, but the meaning of it is personal to him. He might, or might not, even know himself why that number is compelling to him or how it's connected, psychologically, to his behavior."

"That's what I figured, but since the whole psychological thing's not my bailiwick, I thought I'd ask, just in case." He shrugged. "You want that last piece of pizza?"

"Help yourself. I'm full."

"Something else we need to talk about," he said as he scooped up the slice of pepperoni pizza with the long, square tipped fingers that had so sensuously traced patterns on her bare skin, "and that's the suspect list we came up with the other day. Not a single one of the men on that list owns a Chrysler LeBaron. Obviously, we missed someone."

He reached into his back pocket and pulled out a small, spiral bound notebook. The muscles in his jaw bunched as he chewed. Her fingers itched to stroke his stubbled cheek. She closed them around her glass of iced tea. The memory of the feel of his cheek and chin, rough as tree bark with a day's growth of whiskers, leaped into her hand, more real than the smooth, cold glass, until her palm tingled with the recollection of it. She couldn't look away from the cleft in his chin that she wanted to stroke with her thumb.

"Let's go over these again and see if we can figure out what, or who, we're missing." He flipped through the pages and then laid the notebook on the table between them.

She shook her head and refocused on the list they'd compiled. He'd filled the page with his notes. Small, angular writing covered most of the white space.

"Can you decode my shorthand?" He got up and poured both of them more tea, then sat again.

"I think so, yes. Most of it anyway."

"See anything there that surprises you?"

She studied the list and the accompanying notes. Had she known that Joe Bonner, fellow Friday night volunteer at the soup kitchen, was the son of Pastor

William Bonner, founder of Church of the Lamb? She searched her memory. Probably, she decided. Yes, definitely, because she recalled the running joke between Tom Petrie and Joe, that PKs—Preacher's Kids—had to stick together. David Anderson and Darlene McDermott, volunteers at the Day Center for the Homeless were two more PKs. "We're programmed from the cradle to grow up and do good in the world," David had told her.

She looked up at Jack and shook her head.

"You got anything to add that I missed?"

He brushed a crumb from the corner of his mouth, and her gaze followed his hand. She couldn't look at his mouth without remembering how it felt on her, on her lips, on her throat, on her breasts, on her belly, without thinking about the way he tasted, the way he smelled, the delicious friction of bare skin against bare skin, the slow slide of his body into hers. She couldn't look at his mouth without wanting what she couldn't have.

Abruptly she stood and cleared their plates from the table. Standing with her back to him she drew in a deep breath and held it, blinked several times, and slowly exhaled. She wouldn't cry. Not now. Not in front of him.

"What's wrong, Becca?"

His hand on her shoulder was warm. His fingers squeezed gently, and his thumb rubbed small circles on the swell of her upper arm. She wanted to turn around and move closer, rest her head against his chest and let him hold her, pretend she had a right to be in his arms. But she had no such right and it would be dangerous to start lying to herself. She stiffened and stepped away.

"Tell me what's wrong," he ordered. Frustration

sharpened his voice, clipped his words, and whooshed out in a sigh that fanned warmth across the back of her neck.

She intended to tell the truth, however irrelevant, to be firm but vague. She took a deep, fortifying breath, squared her shoulders and turned to face him. Under the bright overhead light his hair shone as golden as the sun. His eyes, the pale blue of an early morning sky, focused on her with single minded resolve.

"We're very different," she began, choosing her words carefully and starting with what she considered to be an obvious, unassailable fact, akin to the sun rises in the east.

"Not so different."

She gaped at him, at a complete loss for words.

"It's a point of honor with both of us that we do what we say we'll do. We're both perfectionists. We both want to be in control." He held up a hand to halt her protest. "Yes, you do, too, you're just nicer about it than I am, and way more tactful. We're both driven. We both feel things deeply and we both conceal our feelings. Both of us are surrounded by other people all day and both of us are lonely." He put a loose fist over his heart. "Here."

She stared at him, stunned. Every single thing he'd said was true. Not that she was going to admit it. But good Lord, he might be the only person on the planet who'd figured some of that out.

"I know the prevailing wisdom is that these things take time, but I know what I want, Becca. I want you."

"We just met a few weeks ago," she objected weakly, groping for the countertop at her back to steady herself. "You don't even know me."

"Sure I do," he said softly. "I may not know your favorite color or who you went to your senior prom with or if you're a Democrat or a Republican, but I know you. I know you're compassionate and generous and loyal. I know you're passionate and stubborn. I know you're totally devoted to the people you love." His eyes darkened, and his voice grew hoarse. "I know the soft sound you make in the back of your throat when you come."

She shoved aside the images that had her breath hitching and her nipples tightening. She blocked out the words that had her heart singing and her resolve melting. Enough of the irrelevant truth. Enough of vague. She drew in a lungful of air and cleared her throat. Time for firm.

"I do not regret the night we spent together, Jack, but we won't be repeating it."

"Now that would be a shame." His voice dropped to a husky note as he moved still closer and trailed the tips of his fingers over her cheek in a slow caress. He slid the palm of his hand to the back of her neck and rested his thumb against the pulse in the hollow of her throat. His hand was velvet warm and heat radiated off his body in waves. "It's the only thing I've done in years worth repeating."

Oh, Lord. Amen to that. She wanted to repeat it right now, this instant, here on the kitchen countertop would be as fine a place as any to melt into him and let him transport her to paradise again. She told herself there'd be no more harm in two nights of magic than in one and for the space of a few seconds she believed it. No, she corrected herself, spending another night with Jack Conroy would be the stupidest thing she could possibly do. She'd already dug herself into a hole she was having a hard time climbing out of; no reason to keep digging.

She stiffened her spine by reminding herself that if he knew she was Millard Harrison's daughter he wouldn't be able to get away from her fast enough. He'd probably trample her getting out the door. She wouldn't see desire in his eyes then. He'd look at her with hatred and revulsion.

But what if he didn't, a little voice in her head asked. What if he accepted her anyway? What if she told him that her father had raped and killed his eight-year-old sister and he still wanted her?

"Not going to happen," she said out loud, not sure even as she spoke whether she was talking to herself or to Jack. The fantasy of confession and absolution ran through her head over and over like a train, endlessly circling the same loop of track: she revealed her true identity and he assured her that it made no difference to him; they kissed. She shook her head to stop the images.

He held her gaze and stroked her throat, lightly caressing the spot where her pulse beat with longing against the pad of his thumb. He gave her a knowing look and a slow smile. Her mouth was so dry she couldn't swallow. She licked her lips and his smile broadened.

"I'll take that as a definite maybe, but not tonight." He slid his hand over her shoulder and down the length of her arm and linked their fingers. His big hand dwarfed her much smaller one. He squeezed and Becca reflexively squeezed back. He grinned, took a backward step, and tugged.

"Come on, walk me to the door. I'll give you another chance soon to kick me out, but tonight I'm leaving under my own steam."

When they reached the front door, Becca disengaged the alarm system and then twisted the knob to swing the door wide. Jack turned toward her and framed her face between his hands.

"While you're thinking about the things I said, think about this, too." He slanted his mouth over hers and gave her a slow, sweet kiss that left her yearning for the impossible when he stepped back and walked away.

****

She was kissing the cop again. It made him sick to his stomach to watch. He couldn't believe he'd misjudged her so badly. He hated being deceived, hated being made a fool of. Anger rose up in him like a clawed beast. He'd turn that beast loose on her soon and slash her to ribbons.

He pictured it in his mind: the knife doing its work, carving the channels through which the red streams of evil would flow from her body. He panted with excitement at the vivid image. Would she plead or fight? He'd bet she was a fighter. He was going to enjoy that.

All the women who had come before her had been nothing more than assignments to be completed. He hadn't chosen a single one of them. He'd done his job, efficiently and with very little passion or enjoyment. True, he'd derived some fleshly gratification, but mostly his satisfaction had come from a job well done, from knowing he'd obeyed God's will.

Becca would be different. She was no stranger. He

knew her. He'd picked her. She was more than just a job to him. She was personal. She'd tricked him and betrayed his trust. She was trying to thwart the plan of the Almighty. She deserved both divine retribution and his. Righteous lust filled his loins, and he knew it was a sign that he had his Father's blessing.

The one the Lord had chosen for him this week was the ultimate test of his willingness to submit himself to the will of his Father. At first he'd thought it was a mistake. He'd almost argued with God and then he remembered how wrong he'd been about Becca. He'd reminded himself over and over that nits grew into lice and all that, but he was still purely dreading it. He wished he could make a substitution and do Becca instead.

Because unlike the nit and all the others who'd preceded her, punishing Rebecca Bennett was going to be pure pleasure.

****

Jack wanted to pound his head against a concrete pillar, tear a brick wall apart with his bare hands, rip a few boulders out of the ground and heave them into the next county. He settled for going to the gym and punishing his body with the free weights. He followed up with five fast uphill miles on the treadmill.

Where had he gone wrong that Becca didn't trust him with the truth? He'd recognized her words for what they were: one big smoke screen. He needed to find out what was she concealing behind the smoke screen. Because whatever it was, that was what needed fixing, not that crap about the two of them being "very different" or not really knowing each other.

He could handle rejection as well as the next guy,

but he hadn't been rejected. He'd been stonewalled. She hadn't said the words that would have sent him on down the road. She hadn't said "I'm not in love with you and I'm positive I never will fall in love with you, Jack" or "the chemistry isn't there for me, Jack" or even a straight out "I don't want to see you again, Jack."

No, she'd said "we're very different" and "you don't really know me." Remembering the shock on her face when he'd detailed some of the ways in which they were alike would have made him laugh except it was so sad. Had none of the people she loved and took care of looked beyond her strength to the loneliness in her heart? Did they all think that because she was strong enough for them to lean on she didn't have any needs of her own? He snorted in disgust with the lot of them.

He didn't know if she could ever fall in love with him, and if he thought about that too long it would freeze the blood in his veins, so he shoved it aside. All he was after now was the opportunity to win her. Chemistry wasn't the problem. If there was one thing he was certain of in all this mess, it was that the fireworks lit up the sky on both sides.

He re-examined their exchange. "You don't really know me" was the crux of the matter. Her voice had dropped and she'd gotten very still, which, he'd observed on other occasions, was what she did when she was scared. What in the world was she so afraid he'd find out? He couldn't conceive what she might have done that was so awful she thought it an insurmountable obstacle. Because he was a cop and she was somehow involved in criminal or illegal activity? He shook his head. That didn't ring true. So, what? In her youth she'd been a drug runner? A porn star? A Grateful Dead groupie? A flimflam scam artist specializing in fleecing old folks of their retirement funds? Those scenarios were so ridiculous he laughed out loud. Hell, he was the one who'd been too busy playing video games to keep his little sister out of the hands of a perverted killer. He didn't imagine she'd done anything that could compete with that.

Well, whatever it was, he was going to find out. He had to know what he was up against if he had any hope of fixing it. He hadn't left tonight because he'd conceded defeat; he damn sure didn't give up that easily. No, he'd beat a tactical retreat in order to think things through and make a new plan. And her earlier comments not withstanding, he was certain she knew him well enough to know that he didn't throw in the towel at the first sign of difficulty. He groaned. God, she'd have dreamed up another slew of arguments when he saw her again. All the more reason for him to be prepared.

First step of the new plan: conduct his own private investigation into Rebecca Bennett's life and background.

Chapter Eleven

Wednesday, February 22nd

Lily O'Brien wasn't supposed to talk to strangers, and that went double when the stranger was a man. Her mother had told her that too many times to count. Mama was probably going to come to the door and call her any minute, and if she got caught with the strange man, she'd be in big trouble. She'd probably have to stay in her room for a month, and no TV, and no friends over to play and no anything else fun.

But the man looked nice and he needed her to help him find his puppy. It was almost dark and his puppy was scared of the dark. Lily was scared of the dark, too; she should have left Amber's house fifteen minutes ago, but they'd been thinking up names for the horse Amber was sure she was going to get for her birthday next month and she hadn't noticed that the sun was going down. The deep shadows were scaring her right now, and that made her feel bad for the puppy.

"She ran down the street that way." The man pointed. "If we walk together, you can look on one side while I look on the other."

"I can only help for a few minutes," she said, "and then I have to go inside, or I'll get it from my mom. What color is your puppy?"

"She's a golden retriever, so she's a blonde, just

like you." He smiled and started walking down the block.

"My cousin, Nick, has a golden retriever. They are so cute. What's her name?" She skipped to catch up with him.

"Bitsy. I'll look on the right and you look on the left. Okay?"

"Okay. Bitsy," she called softly. They were almost to the corner, and she was hoping Bitsy had wandered into Mrs. Stephenson's back yard because already she wanted to be inside her own house where the lights were on, with her mom and her baby sister.

"I think I see her." The man pointed. "By that black car parked at the curb."

The only car at the curb was across the street and almost to the end of the next block. Lily didn't know how he could tell what color it was, she could barely make out the shape of it, that's how dark it had gotten. Hunh-uh, no way. That was too far to go after dark, even for a lost, scared little puppy. She stopped at the curb.

"I hope you find her, I really do, but I have to go back now." She'd actually taken a step backward when he grabbed her.

"You can't quit now, you promised. A deal's a deal, right, Mary?"

"I didn't promise, and my name's not Mary, it's—"

"Li-ly," her mother called. "Lily Ann, you get in the house this minute. One, two—"

"I'm coming, M—" He slapped his hand over her mouth before she could finish. He had both arms pinned to her sides and her feet off the ground. She kicked as hard as she could and she got his knee.

"Li-ly."

Her mother's voice was closer now, and Lily made grunting noises, the only sound she could make with his hand over her mouth. The man ran down the block away from her mother. Lily managed to get her lips open far enough to bite his finger, and she kept kicking for all she was worth. He reached the black car and his grip on her loosened while he got something out of his front pocket. She bucked and squirmed and kicked the side of the car. He popped the trunk open and when she realized he was going to put her in it she twisted one arm behind her and grabbed onto his belt.

"Let her go. Help. Let her go. Let her go. Somebody help." Her mama was screaming bloody murder.

The man whirled around, pried her fingers loose, and flung her straight at her mother, knocking them both to the pavement. She heard the squeal of the tires and looked up just as the car bore down on them.

****

Jack looked at little blonde-haired, blue-eyed Lily O'Brien and saw his sister Megan. Pain squeezed his chest and twisted his stomach into hard knots of fury. He wanted to strangle the son of a bitch who was now preying on children as well as women. He shoved the pain and the anger down and concentrated on the child sitting across the room on her mother's lap. Both of them had cuts, scrapes, and bruises, but were amazingly free of serious injury considering their ordeal.

"You go first, Lily, and your mom will go second. Start at the beginning and tell us what happened." He nodded to include Sully, who'd posted himself by the front door.

He listened intently, first to the daughter and then to the mother. There was no doubt in his mind that the man he was after had tried to kidnap the girl and, failing that, had tried to run her down with his car. Mr. Jergens, who lived on the corner, positively identified the car as a 2006 Chrysler LeBaron and stated he couldn't get the license number because the plate had been covered in mud. The man had called Lily O'Brien "Mary." Lily and her mother were regular church attendees and always sat a few rows back and to the right of the minister's lectern; Jack would bet his bank account that they sat in the fifth row. Lily reported that the man had a ring on the little finger of his left hand and she touched a red place on her chin where she said the ring had pressed against her when he covered her mouth.

Not only Lily and her mother, but Mr. Jergens as well, had clearly seen the man's face. They'd independently described him as muscular, of medium height, maybe five nine or ten (except for Lily, who thought he was huge), with dark brown hair and eyes. All three had agreed to work with the police artist for a sketch to be released to the newspaper and television stations.

Officers were conducting door to door interviews right now. He and Sully would join that effort as soon as they were finished with Lily and her mother, but his hopes were pinned on the sketch. Almost always a sketch produced a flood of calls to the crime tip hotline, and even though most of the tips didn't pan out, often several of them did.

By ten o'clock they'd finished the neighborhood canvas, and there was nothing more they could do that night. Jack climbed into his Jeep and headed to his home that wasn't a home. He hadn't lived in a home since the day Megan—No, he wasn't going there. Time to steer his mind in another direction, and there was no one better at distracting him than his sister, Courtney. By unspoken agreement, they never talked about that night long ago; it was as if there'd always been only the two of them. If he called right now, he could probably get her before she went to bed. She answered on the third ring.

"Hey," he said, "what are you up to?"

"I'm gestating, Jack. Eating everything that isn't nailed down, peeing every five minutes, and watching my feet swell, napping when I can, which isn't nearly often enough because I have to make sure Miranda and Josh don't burn the house down. What are you up to?"

"None of the above, thank God."

She laughed, told him Ben was getting a promotion, reported on the kids' latest doings and reminded him that he was babysitting Sunday evening so she and Ben could celebrate their anniversary. "What's up with you, Jack? How are you?"

"The usual, and I'm fine." As far as anyone in his family knew, he was always fine, even when he wasn't fine. Like now.

"Well, Ben just walked in with a gallon of Rocky Road, God bless him. I'm polishing off a carton every few days lately. We should all buy stock."

After he and Courtney hung up, his mind boomeranged right back to Megan, and this time he couldn't stop the flood of memories. He remembered the last time he'd seen her alive, less than half an hour before she'd been murdered. She'd been wearing white shorts and a pink top and she'd pulled her long, blonde hair into a pony tail. Like Lily O'Brien, she'd been warned numerous times not to talk to strangers. Unlike Lily, no one had chased after her when a man with evil in his heart and a knife in his hand had grabbed her.

He slammed the lid on those thoughts and looked around, surprised to discover that instead of going home he'd somehow ended up at Becca's place. Her bedroom lights were still on, so he wouldn't be waking her if he stopped. He pulled into the driveway behind her Civic and cut the engine. If she took one look at him and threw ice water in his face, it'd be a warmer greeting than he'd get at his apartment. Funny, how he'd craved the silence and solitude of that apartment until Rebecca Bennett had come along. Now the place just seemed empty.

He realized with a start that he'd simply eliminated the sounds of pain from his childhood house and called it good enough. The sound of his mother's angry, slurred speech and his sister's constant, desperately cheerful chatter and the ear splitting acid rock music he'd played nonstop, none of which had been loud enough to drown out the sound of his father's absence. And underneath all of it, at the hollow center of their family, was the unacknowledged but deafening, soul-crushing grief where Megan used to be.

Enough. He plastered his best "I'm fine" face on and rang the bell. Becca answered, wearing a black and red flannel nightgown that covered her from chin to ankle. She took one look at him and pushed the door open.

"What's wrong?"

He stepped inside, wrapped his arms around her

and rested his cheek on the top of her head. Something in his chest loosened, and he could breathe again. He drew in a deep lungful of air and held it, absorbing the dark, musky woman scent of her and holding on tight while his world slowly settled back into place. Her arms closed around his waist. She swayed very slightly from side to side and made a soft humming sound in the back of her throat that wordlessly conveyed comfort, though how she knew he needed it was beyond his ability to guess; no one else had ever seen past his façade. Not even he had known how badly he needed solace until she'd offered it. He gathered her closer, pressed his lips to her hair, and soaked up everything she gave so freely. His stomach unclenched, the tightness in his chest eased, and the muscles in his throat relaxed as he held her.

She was warm and soft and everything good. She fit into his arms perfectly. She filled the hole in his heart. He didn't give a damn what she was hiding; she was everything he needed, everything he wanted, and he'd do whatever was necessary to convince her of that. The minute he got some down time, he'd uncover her secret and get that obstacle out of their way.

She took a step back and led him to the sofa. She flipped on the small lamp beside it and sat, curling her legs under her and pulling her gown over her bare feet. She'd painted her toenails bright cherry red. The nails on her hands were plain. Ah, the hidden facets of Rebecca Bennett. He took a seat beside her, close enough to rest his hand on her knee, and faced her.

"Did he kill another woman tonight?"

"No. He went after a child this time." At the horrified look on her face, he quickly added, "She's okay. She got away."

"Thank God," she whispered.

He told her about Lily O'Brien, smart, brave Lily O'Brien, and her fiercely determined mother. He told her about the results of the door-to-doors and about the police sketch that would be released to the media tomorrow. He'd never talked about his work to anyone except other cops—God knew, no one in his family had ever wanted to hear a word about it—and Becca actually seemed interested. His thoughts kept turning back to Megan, like big black buzzards circling carrion, and every time they did, he told Becca something else about Lily O'Brien.

She was focusing her attention on him in that way she had, intense but undemanding, expecting nothing, accepting anything. The vultures were spinning faster, and the pressure inside him was building again. He talked about Courtney, about her kids, about her pregnancy, about her swollen feet and her craving for Rocky Road ice cream.

"I had another sister. Her name was Megan." The words were out before he could stop them. Once the dam broke, all the memories he'd been holding at bay flooded out. "She was the sweetest person I've ever known, really shy, and boy, did that kid have an imagination. She thought old man Ackerman who lived behind us was a Russian spy. She pretended there was an invisible door behind the piano that was a gateway into another dimension. She carried a notebook around with her and wrote little stories in it, lots of them about fairies. And animals. We had this old, arthritic basset hound that could barely move, and Megan described her in one story as 'a lively dog that raced through the

fields with her ears streaming behind her in the wind.' "
He smiled at the memory. "I don't think Lulu 'raced'
anywhere, ever in her life. I don't think she even
walked fast."

Becca stroked the back of his hand, where it rested
on her knee. He turned his hand over and linked their
fingers. He hadn't said his sister's name out loud in
twenty years, hadn't talked about her to a soul, and now
that he'd started, he couldn't seem to stop the flow of
memories.

"I remember the day they brought her home from
the hospital, all bundled up in a little pink blanket. She
had hair, but she was so blonde that she looked bald. I
swore I'd—" He stopped. He'd sworn he'd beat up
anyone who ever tried to hurt her, but he hadn't done it,
had he? He hadn't protected her when she'd needed it
the most.

"She had me wrapped around her little finger,
that's for sure. I'm probably the only eight year old boy
in the state who regularly got suckered into tea parties,
which was her big thing when she was three. I drew the
line at holding my little finger out, though, just so you
know." He brushed Becca's wrist with his thumb.
"When she was five she decided that pink was her
favorite color, and from then on everything was pink;
pink walls in her bedroom, pink clothes, pink icing on
her birthday cakes, pink barrettes for her hair. Even her
notebooks had to have pink covers. Mom bought her a
purple notebook once, and it threw her into a tizzy you
wouldn't believe."

"Your mom take it back to the store and exchange
it for a pink one?"

"Right away." He'd forgotten how involved his

mother used to be, how she'd joined in all the games and supported them in their various ventures. She'd covered a card table with a red cloth, set it in the front yard and fixed the lemonade they sold from it. She'd taken them to the zoo, to the water park, to the library. She'd made Megan a pink Princess Leia dress and whipped up a black Darth Vader cape for him, fashioned crowns and helmets out of cardboard and painted them. His mom had laughed a lot back then. Before…

"I was supposed to be watching her." He hadn't meant to say that. Only his parents and Courtney knew how badly he'd failed Megan. Becca certainly didn't need to know about it. But that didn't stop the confession from pouring out.

"Mom and Dad were out looking at carpet, and I was in charge of the girls. Courtney was in the den watching *The Last Unicorn* for the millionth time, and I was playing Mario Brothers on the Nintendo. Megan was walking around the house complaining about being bored. She wanted me to take them to the park down the street and I said no. She told me I was a sucky big brother, but she loved me anyway and she was going outside." He swallowed hard. "I said, 'Don't leave the yard, brat.' "

He hated that those were the last words he'd ever said to her. Guilt sat on his chest like a two-ton elephant. This was why he didn't talk about Megan; it hurt too much, and there was nothing he could do to make it better. He couldn't travel back in time and go to the park with her or chase her down the street and make Millard Harrison turn her loose, or even just take his words back.

"The supreme term of affection from a teenage boy. I know this from my experience as a younger sister." Her eyes were liquid pools of understanding. "Did you tug her hair when you said it?"

He had. He'd forgotten until just this minute. She'd stuck her tongue out at him and then spoiled the effect by giggling. The memory was a gift and so was the relief that accompanied it. She hadn't gone to her grave with her feelings hurt because he'd called her "brat."

"What almost happened to Lily O'Brien tonight, that's what *did* happen to Megan. Sick bastard by the name of Millard Harrison raped her and then killed her. Stabbed her seventeen times. Dumped her in the alley like she was nothing, less than nothing." His eyes burned and his throat ached with the effort it took not to break down and cry like a baby. His sweet, sweet Megan, brutalized, murdered, and discarded like so much trash, all because he'd wanted to get to the next level in Mario Brothers.

He surged to his feet and paced the small living room. The roar in his head was deafening. A red haze filled his head and blurred his vision. He wanted to put his fist through the wall, break furniture with his bare hands, smash everything in the room into smithereens. And none of that would change a damn thing.

"You've blamed yourself all these years."

Her voice came to him from a great distance, somehow slipping past the roar of white static to reach him. His gaze locked on her, and his vision cleared. The light from the lamp behind her formed a golden halo above her head.

"I chose a video game over my sister's safety."

"No, you didn't. You chose a video game over the

192

park."

"Same difference."

"Big difference."

"She's still dead." He lowered his voice, which had risen to a shout. "If I'd taken her to the park, she'd be alive."

Guilt pressed down on him until he could no longer stand. He dropped onto the sofa beside her and reached blindly for her hand. Her fingers squeezed his with surprising strength. He closed his eyes and let his head rest against the high cushioned back of the sofa.

"That might be true. And it might not. No way to know for sure." She brushed aside his snort with an impatient shake of her head. "All you can know for certain is that if m—Millard Harrison hadn't been there at that moment in time, she wouldn't have died that day, in that way. That's the big 'if' and all the others are incidental. Believe me, there's plenty of blame to go around. Can't you at least share some of it with the man who actually killed her?"

Jack settled into the silence. Her words rolled through his mind like smooth tumbled stones. She was right. Never mind the "ifs" that had plagued him most of his life: if he hadn't just gotten the new video game, if his parents had been home, if a neighbor had noticed, if Megan had stayed inside. The bulk of the blame lay squarely with Millard Harrison. He opened his eyes, caught her gaze and nodded emphatically.

"I'd have killed the scumbag myself if he hadn't already done the world a favor and hanged himself in prison. I've imagined taking revenge on Millard Harrison a million ways in the last twenty years. I've spit on him and cursed at him. I've strangled him, shot him, lashed him with whips. I've shoved him into a pool of piranhas, staked him to a killer ant hill, tossed him into a rattlesnake pit, buried him alive.

"So, yes, I can share the blame with the sick bastard. And with the doctors who didn't keep him in the hospital where he belonged. And with his family, too. They had to know he was psycho."

She yanked her hand from his with a jerk, pulled her knees up to her chin and curled into a ball. Her face was flushed, her eyes dull. Her sides heaved like she'd run a marathon. Jack stared at her in confusion and then, belatedly, he remembered her brother.

"I'm sorry, Becca. I wasn't thinking." He reached for her, and she drew back. His hand dropped, and then, because he couldn't bear not touching her, because he had to maintain the connection, because he had to give the comfort that she didn't want but clearly needed, came to rest lightly on her leg just above her ankle. "I stomped all over your buttons, huh?"

"You can't possibly know." She gave a weak laugh and a slight shake of her head. He got that buzz just below the surface of his skin, the subdural hum he often got when things started coming together, just before a case broke wide open. He sat forward.

"I can if you tell me."

Every word out of Jack's mouth was like a fist to the gut. Becca curled tighter, as if by so doing she could protect herself from the blows. If he'd actually hit her, it would hurt less. How could she ever tell him now? She should have told him who she was at the very beginning. No, no, she should have kept her distance and never let things get personal between them.

Her chest was on fire and even though she was

gasping for air, she still couldn't seem to take in enough oxygen. The room started to spin and in a distant corner of her mind she realized that she was on the edge of hyperventilating. She forced herself to slow her breathing.

"Talk to me, Becca."

Her mouth was so dry she wasn't sure she could speak even if she wanted to. Which she didn't. And at the same time, she did. When she let the scene of forgiveness she'd been imagining since Monday evening play in her head, she wanted to tell Jack the truth and several times had opened her mouth to do just that. And then the much sharper image of his eyes, filled with contempt and hatred and revulsion as he'd talked about her father, would come into focus and fear would clog her throat until not even the thinnest sound could escape. Did the possibility of understanding and forgiveness outweigh the guilt and shame of a lifetime? Would the truth set her free and open the door to a future with Jack? Or would it bring down the gavel on a life sentence in which he was lost to her forever?

Oh, who was she kidding? He was lost to her now, and she was the one who'd dead bolted the lock on the door. She'd thought she was locking him out, but now saw with stunning clarity that what she'd really done was lock herself in. She was in prison as surely as if she were behind bars, sharing a cell with her secret.

No, her secret was the cell, and it was a damn lonely place. No wonder she hadn't had any real relationships; she hadn't dared to let anyone to know who she was. Even her friendships with other women were one-sided; they confided, she listened. A spurt of anger had her sitting up straight. So what the hell was she doing time for? She hadn't killed anyone. And if Jack Conroy couldn't see that, then he couldn't. But for the first time, she could, and it gave her courage.

She turned toward him. His gaze was riveted on her. His blue eyes were as bright as stained glass with the sun streaming through. Like an electric charge before a storm, the air between them practically crackled with his intensity. He almost vibrated with expectancy.

"Millard Harrison was my father." The sharp hiss of an indrawn breath was his only reaction.

"Charles Bennett adopted me and Kevin after he and our mother married, but Millard Harrison was our biological father."

He removed his hand from her leg to grip his own knee. She wanted to cry at his withdrawal, wanted to grab that hand and hang on, pull him back to her. But his eyes had gone from warm blue to pale ice, and even though his gaze never wavered from hers he seemed to be looking through her to some distant point.

"When he took his medication, and when the medication worked, he was a loving father who read us bedtime stories, built us a tree house, took us camping and fishing and hiking and horseback riding. Other times he was angry and violent, or terrified and withdrawn. He flipped from loving to withdrawn or violent in the blink of an eye. There was never a way to predict the change that any of us ever figured out. One minute he was laughing, the next he was hitting, or breaking things, or kicking holes in the walls, or curled up on the floor of the closet, or throwing one of us across the room. I loved him, and I was scared to death of him."

She'd known it would be terrifyingly difficult to tell Jack about her father; what she hadn't anticipated was how painful it was to remember.

"Kevin and I used to think that aliens from outer space invaded his body, that the fun and loving man was our real daddy and when he was mean and scary, that was the aliens. Red alert—you remember Kevin screaming that at the hospital?"

He didn't respond. She didn't think he was hearing a word she said, but she kept going.

"'Red alert' was code for 'alien invasion.' Even after we knew outer space aliens weren't real, that he had a sickness that made him hear voices in his head and see things that weren't there, 'Red alert' was still shorthand for 'Watch out for Dad; he's hearing the voices again.' Then we learned that we could inherit his illness, and we were both terrified that we'd grow up to be just like him.

"Kevin did become schizophrenic, and then the fear that he'd turn into Dad rode him all the time. That's why he left this last time, a week before his birthday. He turned thirty-three, and that's the age Dad was when—" She stopped. Her burst of anger was long gone. She felt like a defendant on the witness stand, and this was her one and only chance to plead her case. "He was trying to protect all of us, but especially his daughter, Cara."

Jack might have been a statue except for the slight bunching of the muscles in his jaw. Still, she kept talking, a big rushing flood of words, wanting to explain, hoping that if he understood how it had been, he'd be able to separate her from her father in his mind.

"The last time I saw my father I was eight years

old. We were in the kitchen, where we'd been for what seemed like hours, which couldn't have been because Mom just ran to the grocery store, and he was okay when she left, but it felt like forever, with me sitting at the table, no talking, no fidgeting, while he argued with the voices. I'd been scared of him before, plenty of times, but that was the worst. There was something in his eyes." She shuddered and swallowed hard at the image that had haunted her for twenty years.

"I thought he was going to kill me. His eyes were hot and bright, with rage and something else, something I didn't recognize at age eight, but it scared me even more than the rage.

"He'd start toward me with his hands outstretched and that unholy light in his eyes, and then he'd spin away and yell, 'No.' He'd say, 'No, I won't do it,' and 'No, she's not part of this,' and 'No, she's my daughter, I won't.' After ten or twelve times of this, he did grab me. Kevin jumped on his back and yelled at him to let me go. He knocked Kevin clear across the room and then he hugged me real tight for the longest time. Finally, he yelled 'No' again and slung me across the room, too, and then he ran out of the house.

"And then he raped and killed another little girl instead of me. Megan. He raped and killed your sister, Megan, instead of me."

His silence was crushing. Because she knew what it was. It was condemnation that hadn't been put into words yet. The defendant had been found guilty.

Jack stared at Becca in disbelief. Surely he hadn't heard her right, because she'd said…she'd said…Oh, God. A charge of adrenaline jolted him to his feet. She tilted her head back to meet his gaze.

"Your father was *Millard Harrison*?" He willed her to deny it, but she nodded. Anger rose, hot and hard, until he thought his chest was going to explode.

"I can't believe you kept that little detail to yourself." He ground the words out through clenched teeth. "You are a piece of work. A lying, conniving piece of work." His eyes narrowed as realization struck him.

"You thought your brother was the one raping and killing women, didn't you?"

She nodded and opened her mouth to speak, but he cut her off with a slash of his hand through the air. He didn't want to hear what she had to say. He couldn't believe a word that came out of her mouth. She'd lied to him. God, what a fool he'd been.

"You got friendly with me to get information so you could warn him if we got too close, that it? Anything to keep your brother out of prison, right? Even the horizontal cha cha with the cop on his case." He hardened his heart against the hurt in her eyes.

"I was not trying to keep Kevin out of prison. I—"

"Save your breath," he interrupted. "I get it. Lie to me, use me, and then get rid of me—that pretty much sum up your plan?" He grabbed his jacket from the arm of the sofa, strode to the door and jerked it open. "Consider it done."

****

He'd failed.

He couldn't believe everything had gone so horribly wrong. He went over it and over it in his mind, trying to identify the flaw in his execution.

His target shared a room with her sister who was barely more than a baby, not even out of diapers yet, and he'd prayed that it wouldn't be necessary for him to harm an innocent. He'd actually had a nightmare that he'd had to kill the baby, too. So he'd recognized it as divine intervention right away when he'd seen the girl coming down the street toward him, and he'd seized the opportunity God had given him. Snatching her outside seemed a lot less risky all the way around than going into the house for her later that night after everyone had gone to bed.

The story about the lost puppy had been a stroke of genius, if he did say so himself, and she'd bought right into it. So why had she balked at the corner? He saw now that he shouldn't have grabbed her then; he'd scared her and he was too far from the car to get her into it without drawing attention to himself. He should have used persuasion instead of force, like "Oh, no, I think my puppy is hurt. Help me get her into the car." Why hadn't he thought of that?

Because he was so upset by Becca's betrayal, that's why. Since he'd seen her kissing the cop again on Monday evening, he'd been able to think of little else. She'd not only betrayed him by turning his letter over to the cop, she was betraying him by sinning with that same cop. And to think he'd once believed her to be good and pure and true. He'd actually harbored the hope that God meant for her to be his.

Rage rose in him, fast and hot. She wasn't worthy of him. A Jezebel, that's what she was. No, not a Jezebel, *a Mary*. Becca was just another Mary, deserving of punishment. It was his divine right and his great personal pleasure to be the instrument of God's retribution and deliver that punishment. She'd cut his mission short, and in so doing she'd hastened her own

Judgment Day.

The cops would be closing in on him soon. Both the girl and her mother had seen his face. He'd already put the LeBaron back in the big garage and retrieved his own car. That should buy him a little time, and a little was all he needed to send Rebecca Bennett to hell.

Chapter Twelve

Wednesday, February 22nd

Tears blurred her vision as Becca watched Jack Conroy, spine stiff with anger, walk out of her house, out of her life. The door closed behind him with a quiet click of finality. And that was that. Exactly what she'd expected. Her chest tightened against the ache that radiated outward from her heart and spread to every cell in her body. She wrapped her arms tightly around her bent legs, dropped her forehead to her knees, and let the tears flow.

He'd never be able to forgive her for being Millard Harrison's daughter, and how ironic was that because tonight for the first time in her life, she'd forgiven herself. For twenty years she'd carried the twin burdens of guilt and shame; guilt that Megan Conroy had wrongly died in her place, and shame that she was glad to be alive, as if she had been the one to choose which of them would live and which would die. Tonight she'd seen the truth, and even though the anger was long since gone, the truth remained: she'd had no control and none of it was her fault. Not her father's mental illness, not the inadequacies of the mental health system or the limitations of medical science, not the murder of Megan Conroy.

And the universe was a bitch on steroids because

she'd fallen in love with a man for whom the sight of her face would be a reminder of his worst nightmare. He wouldn't be able to look at her without seeing her father and his dead sister and his own fallibility and, of course, her deception.

A sob tore loose from deep in her belly and then another and another, a hard, roiling boil of sobs. Pain gripped her in its brutal fist, so tight and cold that spasms of shivers rippled through her like icy needles, sharp and stabbing.

The squeak of the door hinges came to her from far away. She lifted her head and stared, uncomprehendingly, at the man standing in her doorway. The knife in his hand glinted silver. He grinned.

"Judgment Day, Mary."

****

Jack gripped the steering wheel in both hands and squeezed. By force of will, he kept his foot from bearing down on the accelerator, held it at a nice, even thirty-five miles an hour, which was the posted limit, when what he wanted was to hit warp speed. He had no destination in mind except *away*. He wanted as far away from Rebecca Harrison Bennett as he could get.

His heart hammered in his chest like an angry fist, hard and fast. Adrenaline pulsed through him in scorching hot waves, and he couldn't catch his breath. *Talk about your sucker punch. Why didn't you just gut stab me, Becca? It would have been quicker and less painful.*

He reached Riverside Drive and stopped, unable to make the decision whether to go north or south. Because it didn't matter. He wasn't going anywhere but away. When a car pulled up behind him, he turned north.

Millard Harrison's daughter, he kept repeating. It didn't seem real to him, but he knew it was true. *That* was her big secret, the one he'd been sure wouldn't be an obstacle. *That* was what she'd meant when she'd said he didn't really know her. Boy, she'd had that right. Fifteen minutes ago he'd have bet his bank account that he knew everything about her that he needed to know, everything that really mattered. And he'd be penniless, too.

Millard Harrison's daughter, he thought again, and again her duplicity was a knife to the stomach. He'd fallen, like the proverbial ton of bricks, for Millard Harrison's daughter. Did the universe have a sense of humor or what? All that time he'd been spilling his guts to her, telling her about Megan, and she already knew.

A fresh surge of anger had him slamming his fist into the dashboard. She could have stopped him a dozen times, but had she? No. She'd let him break a twenty-year silence about Megan only to inform him after the fact that he'd bared his soul to the woman whose father had murdered her.

He managed, finally, to draw in a deep lungful of air, and then another, and some of the heat went out of him. After he'd taken several more deep breaths, his head began to clear.

Okay, truth be told, if that bastard were his father, he'd keep mum about it, too. So, if their positions were reversed, when would he have told? He sure wouldn't have announced it upon meeting her. "Hi, I'm Jack, and my father killed your brother. How can I help you?" No way. Mentally, he reviewed the time they'd spent together. Her aloofness, her efforts to keep things between them on a professional level, the mixed messages—it all made sense now. And they'd found her brother a week before they'd made it into the bedroom, so that had not been her motivation for having sex with him. A knot in his stomach unraveled when he put that together.

Monday evening, he decided, when he was pushing her for the real reason she was sending him on his way, would have been the perfect opportunity. Monday evening. Two days ago.

He'd whacked out over what was, in retrospect, a two day difference between when he thought she should have told him and when she'd actually told him. If he was going to be honest with himself, and he always was, he'd have to admit that the "lying" had just been a handy excuse, an acceptable reason for him to get mad and leave. The real problem was that she was *Millard Harrison's daughter*. That was what he couldn't wrap his mind around, couldn't get past. It was just too weird.

He was a block away from the station when he realized that was where he was going. Fitting, too, because he had a killer to catch. Rebecca Bennett had him all jammed up, and the best thing he could do for himself right now was to quit thinking about her and focus on getting that murdering scumbag off the streets.

His attacks had come once a week, every Wednesday evening, for eight weeks. If his pattern held, they had seven days in which to nail him before he struck again.

But his pattern wouldn't hold, Jack realized. His pattern had been broken when Lily O'Brien had gotten away from him. He'd be enraged by that and he'd be looking for another victim, someone to take that rage out on. He'd be driven to compensate for his failure by killing another woman as soon as possible. Maybe even tonight. *Probably* tonight. Dammit.

Re-examining what he knew for certain, he pulled into a parking slot right outside the station door. He got his victims' names and addresses on Sunday morning off the friendship pad at a church. He drove a 2006 black Chrysler LeBaron, two door, hard top. He attacked on Wednesday evening, between the hours of seven p.m. and midnight.

How would he choose a new victim now? Did he have a back up name in reserve? Would he pick a stranger? A woman he knew? The hair on the back of Jack's neck stood up.

He knew Becca.

He'd singled her out, written her a letter, explained his crimes, and reassured her of her safety. Jack suspected his real motivation had been to win her admiration and maybe even her blessing. Becca had turned the letter over to the police. If he knew that, he'd feel betrayed and that would further enrage him. It was a small step in distorted logic from betrayal to blame for his failure with Lily O'Brien and an even smaller step from blame to revenge or, as he'd put it in his letter, punishment.

Unbidden, mental pictures of the slashed and mutilated—punished—bodies of Juliet Crouch, Lillian Robinson, and Heather McCall came into his mind, followed by an image of Becca as the latest victim, body broken and disfigured, that sucked all the air out of him and turned the blood in his veins to ice.

In that instant, it was clear to him that Becca had been Millard Harrison's victim, too; not a co-conspirator by virtue of birth, but a victim. Shame rolled through him as he recalled his reaction to her revelation about her father. He'd lumped them together, but Becca was not her father, and she was in no way responsible for Megan's death. She'd been his victim as surely as had Megan, every day of her life for the first eight years.

He hoped he was wrong, that another madman wasn't about to set his demons loose on her, that the killer wouldn't turn on Becca, but his gut told him otherwise. Frantically, he jammed the key back into the ignition, slammed the Jeep into reverse, and prayed he wouldn't be too late.

****

"Hi, Joe." Becca pretended she didn't see the knife. She resisted the almost overwhelming urge to jump up and make a run for it. But he stood between her and the front door, and if she tried to reach the back door he'd get to her before she got to it. She suppressed a shudder at the image of being tackled from behind. Intuition and experience told her that fear would excite him so she kept hers carefully hidden.

"Come on in." Her nonchalant greeting rattled him; he shifted his weight from one foot to the other and his gaze darted nervously around the room.

"Have a seat." She gestured at the chair next to the sofa.

She tugged at the hem of her nightgown, freeing her feet. She'd try talking and listening, but if worse came to worst and they ended up in a physical struggle, she did not want to pit her upper body strength against his. Unlike a man, a woman was stronger in her legs than her arms. That was one of the few things she remembered from the self-defense class she'd taken ten years ago.

"You want something to drink?" If he fell for that she had a prayer of getting out the back door. "Coffee? Iced tea? Pop?"

"Shut up. Just shut up." He advanced on her slowly, purposefully. He stopped when one more step would have had him bumping into the edge of the sofa. He stood, looming over her, and breathing hard. His eyes glittered as he brought the knife up with a quick jerk, halting an inch from her face.

"You've been very bad, Mary."

She recognized the unholy light in his eyes; she'd seen it in her father's that last time, the time she'd known he was going to kill her. Her reaction was the same now as then. An eerie calm stole over her. She was a detached observer, registering everything, feeling nothing. Rapidly, she sifted through options and weighed probable outcomes.

"Tell me how I've been bad, Joe." The more he talked, the more information she'd have, and the right information was a weapon as powerful as the knife he held in his fist.

"You chose him over me," he shouted. Something in his voice, in the tilt of his head, in the slight quiver of his lower lip, was like a hurt, bewildered little boy. So now she knew that the real target of his rage was a woman who'd had power over him as a child and who had abandoned him in favor of a man, probably a man who abused him. The odds were that woman was his mother, but maybe it had been a baby sitter or a Sunday school teacher or a neighbor or a scout leader or a coach's wife; the possibilities were manifold.

"I'm sorry she let him hurt you. That was very wrong."

Relief, confusion, skepticism, and anger raced across his features in rapid succession. Abruptly, his expression hardened. His eyes narrowed, his lip firmed, his jaw tightened.

"But you won't do it again." He nicked the end of her chin and smiled in satisfaction. "You have sinned for the last time."

"You were so little, and he was so big. You couldn't stop him, but she could have."

Again, he looked like a hurt, scared little boy, badly in need of comfort. And again, just as quickly, rage flared.

"You have interfered with God's plan and betrayed His servant for the last time." Slowly, deliberately, he drew the knife across her cheek and stared, mesmerized by the blood that ran down her neck.

"Look at me, Joe." She had to interrupt the trance he was in, had to pull him out of it. "Look at me, Joe," she commanded. "I'm Becca. *Look at me.*"

He blinked, dragged his gaze away from the blood, and fixed his eyes on hers. Good. She had to keep him focused on her, had to get him to see *her*.

"I'm Becca," she repeated. "You didn't deserve to be hurt. It wasn't your fault that he did what he did. I'm sorry she didn't protect you."

"He got so mad," he whispered. "I forgot to close the cereal box. I spilled my milk. I ran in the house. I turned the TV up too loud. I left my shoes in the living room. I didn't pick up my toys. I didn't eat my peas."

His eyes glazed over and he swallowed convulsively. "I hate peas," he whined. Bad sign. He'd regressed to helpless child, and rage was sure to ride in to the rescue.

"I hate peas, too," she said. "I hated them when I was a kid, and I still hate them now that I've grown up. You still hate them now that you've grown up?"

He didn't answer, but his eyes focused on her again. His grip on the knife had relaxed.

"All those things—spilling milk, running in the house, leaving your toys out—all children do those things. Those are normal kid things, Joe."

"He hit really hard, and his hands were huge."

He wore the unfocused stare that told her he'd regressed again. The hand holding the knife shook. Time to bring him back to the present, remind him that he was big now and try to separate herself from his mother in his mind.

"You didn't deserve any of it. You were just a child then. I wish your mother had kept you safe when you were little, Joe."

He let go of a bark of laughter that scraped across her skin like rusted metal. Her legs tensed in readiness.

"I think it turned her on. He'd beat me and she'd stand there crying like his fists were slamming into her, then he'd drag her into their room, and I could hear them going at it like dogs. After he went to sleep, then she'd come check on me, but she always spread her legs for him first." He made a sound like an animal growl, and spittle sprayed from his mouth.

"She should have kept you safe, Joe."

"She's a whore," he shouted, his face purple with rage. "And you're just like her. You chose that cop over me, and you think I don't know what you've been doing with him? You think I don't know how you've been sinning? God's punishment for sin is death. Judgment Day, Mary."

Now, Becca told herself and she kicked upward with her legs, aiming her heels at his crotch, just as he stabbed downward with the knife.

****

Jack took the corner onto Becca's street on two wheels. As the Jeep fishtailed and then righted itself, he flipped off the emergency portable flashers, popped open the glove compartment to grab a pair of handcuffs, and cut his speed. If, indeed, the killer was here it wouldn't do to advertise his arrival. Had Becca locked the door and reset the alarm after he'd left? God, he hoped so. He didn't see a black Chrysler LeBaron anywhere around, and that didn't mean a damn thing.

Silently, he slid the Jeep to the curb two doors down from Becca's, yanked the key out of the ignition, and hit the ground at a dead run. He kept to the shadows, pulled his Sig Sauer from the shoulder harness, and thumbed off the safety as he approached her porch at an angle.

His pulse spiked at the sight of the front door, slightly ajar. He knew he'd pulled it firmly shut behind him, and if Becca had reset the alarm she'd have locked it first. He took both steps in one leap and edged the door wider with his toe. The sight that greeted him chilled him to the bone.

The man who slashed at Becca with a bloody knife was in such a frenzy he didn't realize he had company. Jack couldn't get a shot off without risking hitting Becca, who aimed a feeble kick at her assailant. With a roar he launched himself across the room, knocking the man to the floor, and pinning him in place with a knee in the small of his back. In seconds he'd twisted the other man's arm until he dropped the knife, jerked both arms behind his back, and snapped the handcuffs around his wrists.

"Becca?"

"I'm fine." She gave him a wobbly smile, and then she passed out.

****

Sully had beaten the ambulance by seconds. Jack had turned Joe Bonner over to him and ridden in the ambulance with Becca to the hospital.

He'd never felt more helpless in his life than when he stood to the side of the emergency room cubicle while medical personnel swarmed over Becca, taking vital signs, starting a second IV for transfusing blood, cleaning wounds. She lay still and unmoving at the center of all the activity. Except for the reddish-brown ribbons of dried blood on her chin and her left cheek, her face was almost as white as the sheet underneath her.

Fear constricted his chest until he struggled to breath, squeezed his throat with a cold fist, sent his heart rate into overdrive. He'd almost lost her, might still. Without her, his life would be as sterile and colorless as this white and stainless steel room. Why had he thought, even for a second, that it mattered who had fathered her?

Although Doctor Ellenburg had asked him and then ordered him to leave the room, Jack had refused to budge. The doctor finally gave up, seated himself on a rolling stool at her feet, and painstakingly began suturing the multitude of cuts and gashes that Joe Bonner had inflicted on Becca.

Jack ignored the tubing, the machines that beeped and hissed, the shiny needles, the yards of gauze, the miles of stitches and the nurses who crisscrossed the room on rubber-soled shoes. He watched the shallow rise and fall of Becca's breasts, the rapid flutter of her pulse in the hollow of her throat, the occasional twitch of her bloody legs, and willed her to live.

"She'll be fine," Dr. Ellenburg assured him, gripping his right arm just above the elbow and giving it a reassuring squeeze. "She's stabilizing. We've stopped the bleeding, and we're giving her antibiotics to prevent infection. We'll push fluids for the next several hours and replenish her blood supply. The pain medication is going to keep her drowsy; we'll start backing off on it tomorrow and see how she does. We're moving her upstairs now."

"I'll go with her," Jack stated firmly without shifting his gaze away from Becca. He almost didn't believe it when she opened her eyes, but then she looked right at him, and smiled. Before he could respond, her eyelids had drifted closed again. It wasn't much, but it was enough that he could finally breathe.

When Becca was settled in her room, he reluctantly relinquished his post at her side to Marie Bennett, who had been waiting in the room for her daughter.

"Thank you so much," she said to him. "Thank you for saving her." She gave him a hug and rose on tiptoe to kiss his cheek.

Jack felt like a fraud. If he hadn't gotten mad and stormed out, Becca wouldn't have been attacked in the first place.

He backed out of the room and headed toward the parking lot, where Sully had promised he'd have an officer bring the Jeep. Time to get to the station and wrap things up with Joe Bonner. Or, more accurately, wrap up Joe Bonner, so tight he'd never see the light of day, never have a chance to hurt another woman, never again be a threat to Becca.

****

Thursday, February 23rd

Becca floated, weightless, in a dark, quiet place. She wondered briefly where she was, but she didn't care enough about the answer to open her eyes and look. She liked it here, wherever here was. She wanted to stay here forever. Except...

The barest ripple of awareness fanned her face with a feather soft caress, and she grew conscious of a dim light glowing high above her. She drifted upward, closer to it, and now she heard the faint hum of, what? There was a word for it, but she couldn't think what it was. Didn't matter. Something—the, the, voices, that was the word—called to her, and she rose higher. Odd, how the higher she rose, the heavier she felt. The light glowed brighter and brighter, welcoming her. The voices grew louder, clearer: her mother's voice and Jack's. Jack was on the other side of the light! She needed to tell him something. She couldn't remember what, but she knew it was important.

She rose faster and then stopped abruptly as pain slammed into her and spun her around. She was on fire. Her whole body screamed in agony. Immediately she spiraled downward, sinking quickly back into the dark, away from the light, away from the voices, away from the pain.

Her next awareness was the sensation of vibrating. She willed it to go away and it did. The light was closer this time, and slowly, cautiously, she began to rise toward it. As she did, the mist in her mind began to melt away and memories of the night before took shape: Jack at her door. His stories about Megan. Her confession. His anger. His leaving. Her tears. Joe Bonner. The knife.

She burst into the light and the last memory formed: Jack had come back. She opened her eyes, and there he was.

Spikes of golden hair stood out at his temples as if he'd been pulling at it. His square jaw, covered in rough stubble, was clenched, and his thin lips formed a tight, straight line. His pale blue eyes were rimmed in red and surrounded by bruise-like shadows. He looked even more the avenging angel she'd imagined him to be that first time he'd shown up at her office. Now she knew better. Now she knew him for who he was. Not an avenging angel, but a mortal man.

But Jack Conroy, with his big heart and his hard head, was no ordinary man. He was a man driven by demons, a doggedly determined man, a difficult man. He was also a man you could count on, a man you could trust, a man who used his strength to shelter and protect. And he was the man she loved.

"Becca," her mother said, squeezing her left hand. "Oh, thank God, you're awake."

"About damn time." Kevin patted her right shoulder.

Her gaze was locked on Jack, who stood still as a statue at the foot of her bed. She gave him a tentative smile. His expression remained unchanged. Well, what had she expected? It was the cop who'd saved her, not the man. He probably wanted to take her statement and get out of here. He was, after all, surrounded by Millard Harrison's family. She might as well do the merciful thing for both of them and speed his departure.

"Mom, Kevin," she said, still looking at Jack. "I love you both. Help me sit up a little, and then please give me and Detective Conroy some privacy."

"Oh, my God. It's him." Kevin punched up the volume on the remote to the television on the wall above Jack's head. Joe Bonner's face filled the screen.

"Just after midnight, Joseph Nathaniel Bonner was arrested, charged, and jailed without bail on six counts of rape, two counts of first degree murder, one count of attempted murder, and one count of attempted kidnapping. Against the advice of his attorney, Scott Nesbitt, Mr. Bonner has confessed to all of the charges brought against him. Channel Two's Jill Younger is with his parents, the Reverend and Mrs. William Bonner. Jill."

"Cindy, I have with me Pastor William Bonner, of Church of the Lamb, and his wife, Mary." The dark-eyed reporter looked somberly into the camera and then the lens widened to include William and Mary Bonner. William Bonner had aged ten years since Becca had seen him a week and a half ago. Grief pinched his features, bracketed his mouth with deeply carved lines, and leached the color out of his face. Becca's heart went out to him.

"What was your first thought upon learning that your son confessed to the crimes of multiple rapes and murders?"

"What I thought—what I know—is that it's my

fault, Jill. Before the Lord laid His hand on me, I was more monster than man. Like my father before me, I was a bitter, angry man, who thought that life wasn't fair, the world treated me badly, and no one gave me the respect I deserved. Rage festered inside me like a cancer. And who did I take it out on? My wife and my son, that's who. I beat them both, often. My fists were brutal and my tongue was vicious. Joe lived with fear and pain and humiliation during the formative years of his life. On his fifth birthday, I beat him for smearing the icing on his chocolate birthday cake on the tablecloth. That very night the Lord touched my heart and changed me, but the damage to Joe had already been done. In Exodus, chapter 34, verse seven, the Bible tells us that the sins of the fathers shall be visited on the children unto the third and fourth generations, and that's exactly what I've done. The sins my father visited upon me, I visited upon my son."

"Mrs. Bonner, what is your reaction to the fact that your son drove your car during the commission of his crimes?"

The camera zoomed in for a close up shot of a pale, dark-haired, dark-eyed woman.

"I love my son," she said. "I pray that God forgive him and us." She burst into tears and collapsed against her husband's chest.

"Back to you, Cindy."

Becca glanced at Jack, who hadn't moved a muscle, whose expression remained inscrutable and whose gaze was still locked on her.

"Mom, Kevin, on the count of three," she reminded them.

The pain in her legs when they scooted her up was

excruciating, but it was nothing compared to the pain in her heart. Whoever the idiot was who said it was better to have loved and lost than never to have loved at all had been smoking something seriously illegal at the time he came out with that rubbish.

She'd closed her eyes against the pain, and when she opened them, Jack had moved to the side of the bed. He stared at her for a long, silent moment and then reached out a hand and cupped the side of her face. He lightly traced around the stitches in her chin and cheek with his thumb. The gesture, so gentle and unexpected, made her heart stutter and then leap with hope.

"Forgive me," he said, his voice low and hoarse. "Forgive me for the ugly things I said. I know none of it is true. You're not a liar, not a user, and you would never help a rapist stay free to rape again, even if he were the brother you love."

His thumb stilled, and he took a deep, shuddering breath. His shoulders shook as if he were straining under a great weight. Becca pressed her cheek into his palm and covered his hand with her own.

"It's okay, Jack."

"Sshh. It's not okay. Let me finish. I'm just getting started." The corner of his mouth twitched upward in a self- deprecating smile. "I've had all the hours you've been lying in this hospital bed to figure some things out. I'm so sorry I got mad and stormed out and left you a sitting duck for Joe Bonner."

"Jack," she interrupted, but he stilled her with his thumb on her lips.

"It's not your turn yet. Thing is, I've built my life around hating your father. That hate has pretty much defined who I am. Some would say that's a dangerous thing, and they'd probably be right, but mostly it's an empty thing. I didn't realize how empty, until you."

His eyes filled with tears, and the sight made her own burn, put a lump in her throat, and filled her chest with tenderness. He made no effort to blink away the tears or to hide them from her.

"What hate does, is it hollows you out inside. I've been an empty shell of a man, Becca, until you. You fill me up. Because I love you. I don't have to hold onto that hate anymore, because I've got something a whole lot better."

Tears coursed down his face, ran through the stubble on his cheeks, fell in big warm drops from his chin onto her bare arm. Her own eyes swam.

"So what I'm asking is, can you forgive me, and will you give me another chance to earn your love?"

"Yes," she said, turning her face slightly to press a kiss into his palm. "I forgive you. And I hope you'll forgive me, too. I should have told you who I really was much earlier."

"Sshh," she said when he started to object. "It's not your turn." He smiled. She caught his arm and pulled him closer.

"Love doesn't have to be earned. It's a gift, freely given, and already yours. I love you, Jack, with everything I am and ever will be. But there's something I have to know." She framed his face with her hands.

"Look at me, Jack. Can you look at me without seeing my father? Without seeing Megan? I need to know what you see when you look at me." She held her breath as he studied her. His hands came up to cradle her head.

"I see everything," he whispered. "Everything I

want. Everything I need. Everything that matters. Life. Love. A home."

His lips brushed hers softly, once, twice, and then his mouth settled firmly over hers. She tasted his tears and his love, his sweetness and his strength. She breathed in the air he exhaled and gave him back her own.

The sound of a throat clearing interrupted them. Becca looked over Jack's shoulder and saw an older, gray-haired man in a doctor's white jacket standing in the doorway.

"Time to unhook you," he said as he came into the room.

Jack edged toward the head of the bed, moving only far enough to allow the doctor room to remove the IV, and stepping back to Becca's side while the doctor wrote out prescriptions and gave her care instructions for her legs.

"I'm going to discharge you, but you're going to need someone to take care of you."

"She's got me," Jack said to the doctor, still looking at Becca.

"I've got him." Becca smiled at Jack. "Let's go home."

A word about the author...

Catherine S. Morgan lives in Oklahoma. As a clinical social worker, she has had wonderful and often heroic clients, many of whom have suffered unimaginable trauma. She has worked with abused children, delinquent teenagers, rape victims and battered women, people struggling with depression, anxiety, post traumatic stress, and personality disorders. Violence against women and children is epidemic, and the damage done goes far beyond the immediate victims; indeed its reverberations are felt throughout our society.

You can learn more about Catherine and her writing at catherinesuemorgan.com or on Facebook at www.facebook.com/cathy.morgan.7739